NO

MERCY

JAYE CHERÍE

ISBN: 978-1-7320583-1-6

ISBN-13: 978-1-7320583-0-9

BOOKS BY JAYE CHERÍE

THE GOLDDIGGER'S CLUB
THE COST OF LOVE AND SANITY
ALL GOLD NO GLITTER

ACKNOWLEDGMENTS

I would like to thank God for always putting a vision in my mind and a story in my heart. I'd also like to thank my beta readers for their priceless feedback. Last but not least, to readers, you make the world go round. I hope this book sparks more important conversations about women and sexual rights for all.

Prologue

yron Mercy furiously rubbed at the tear in his chair. The furniture was supposed to be more durable. He bought it to look like something out of a European palace. Everything he owned was supposed to exhibit taste and wealth. He belonged. Though he was the "young man" in the community, he fit in, even with the older men who stood around talking with Cuban cigars hanging from their lips, turning their noses up. At times, the old heads excluded him from special events because they didn't think he was proper. Sure, he had edge, courtesy of his wild ties to the music industry, but he was focused on his life in Westbrook, Florida, a small town on the outskirts of Tampa.

His custom-renovated mansion sat on the hill in the conservative neighborhood, twenty miles from his poorer beginnings. He'd joined the right circles with the right people. Everything was just right, except for when it came to his daughter, Erica. Nothing he did made her right. Up until recently, he had no real clue how wrong she was.

He knew Erica was no virgin. He suspected it long before he started hearing rumors in the industry about her. Byron never asked her because it wasn't something he wanted to know. If it were true, what was he going to do about it? Ground her for life? Spank her? She wasn't his little girl anymore. He certainly couldn't go after the engineers and producers, not outright anyway. He needed to keep his career going. But there were a few people wondering why some of their music collaborations and business deals fell through. That would be Byron's doing. As for Erica, she would deny everything, until now.

Though Byron's back was turned to the door, he could hear someone step lightly into the room. He knew it was her. She did that a lot lately, especially over the last eight months.

"Daddy," Erica Mercy said.

"What?" Byron continued to examine the couch with his hand.

She didn't respond right away, which irritated him. He scowled. "What do you want?"

"I know what I want to do with it," she said.

Byron waited to hear more. He heard her step forward. "I want to give it up for adoption."

"It's too late."

"Why?"

Byron finally turned to face his daughter. She wore a black and white dress that hugged her large baby bump. Her dark hair was brushed back. He didn't bother to hide the displeasure on his face as she looked at him with almond-shaped eyes. "You waited too long. The process takes months. It'll be two years old before we get it out of here. What were you thinking? That you could take care of it? Be a good mother? You can't even take care of yourself."

Erica touched her stomach. Byron diverted his eyes, preferring not to concentrate on her maternal gesture.

"I don't want it," she said.

"Neither do I," Byron mumbled, brushing his hand over his goatee.

"Can't we give it to somebody?"

"How about the man you made it with?"

It was Erica's turn to drop her gaze.

"When are you going to be honest with me, little girl?"

She shook her head. "I won't talk about it."

"Really?"

"It doesn't matter. He's a nonissue."

"When I find out who it is, he's got something coming to him."

Byron heard the patter of liquid hitting his floor. He looked to see water leaking from between her legs.

"Veronica!"

Chapter 1

Back on the Saddle

The IV sticking out of Erica's arm itched like crazy. She scratched it lightly. A nurse walked through the hospital room door carrying a bundle. A soft cry came from the well-wrapped blanket as she placed the newborn baby in Erica's arms. It cooed. For a brief minute, she'd forgotten about the anguish its birth caused—but only for a minute. She noticed that the baby's arms were deformed. When she looked at its face, the child stared at her with yellow-green snake eyes. Erica started to feel sick to her stomach.

"Are you OK?" the nurse asked. She reached to grab the baby away from Erica. There was no protest. The door opened again, and this time her father and stepmother walked in.

Erica gasped and woke up from the horrible dream at home in her bedroom. She heard the eight-month-old crying in the distance and heavy footsteps rushing in the opposite direction. Sounded like Lana, the house help, tending to Erica's baby. She was still waiting for someone to take the child off her hands. She couldn't bear the thought of keeping a reminder of her rape. She sighed at the return to her uncomfortable reality. Of course, her dreams weren't much better. They ended with something crazy almost every night. It made her want to skip sleep altogether. She never slept the whole night anyway.

Perhaps it was guilt. She never thought she'd be the type to give her child away, but there was nothing else she could do. Erica briefly thought she'd be able to handle the stress. These bad dreams showed her different. She told herself the girl would be better off with someone else. Then she'd wonder if her mother thought the same thing. The very comparison made her hair curl. She was nothing like her mother, who so carelessly left and forgot all about her. *She* was worse. Erica had negative experiences that led her to this decision. Her mother, on the other hand, was selfish.

Erica lay in bed on her back and stared at the ceiling. It was the same high ceiling she'd stared at since she was fourteen. She asked Daddy if she could paint it. He answered with a booming "no." He wouldn't allow her to ruin his house. She would only want to change it soon anyway, he said. Daddy was right. She changed her mind often. Was there anything wrong with that? There was, according to him.

The sound of crying stopped. She rolled over and watched the sunrise shine its rays throughout the large room. Even though her blinds were still closed, the light peeked through as much as it could. She finally hit a button on her remote, and the blinds slid back, revealing windows across half the room. She could see lush, green hills in the distance. There wasn't a house in sight—the way her father liked it. When she was tired of staring out the window, she tossed her fluffy, white comforter off and pushed herself out of bed.

Erica looked in the mirror at her figure. No one looking at her would ever know that she had been pregnant. Her five-foot-six-inches, 120-pound frame made it easy for her to find flattering clothing. While some would say she had an average face, she didn't feel average. If in a room with other women, she had no problem dominating the attention of the most eligible bachelor.

Erica pulled herself together and sauntered downstairs wearing a white, see-through V-neck top over some ripped jeans. She had decided to switch her hairstyle and wear it straight and shoulder-length. She smoothed the black strands of hair evenly to the side.

The first person she saw was her father. He was on his phone, waving for her to follow him. She did. He led her into his office. The soft light complemented the wooden décor. There were rows of books that Daddy never read and a globe sitting on the coffee table in front of a green and eggshell sofa. The shiny, wooden conference table housed five executive chairs. They weren't the stuffy ones you see in retail stores—these were plush and comfortable. Of course, there was that one chair bigger than the others—no doubt a place for the master of the house.

Erica glared at the bassinet in the middle of the floor with bags around it. She diverted her eyes away. Why did her father bring her in here? She didn't want any part of the arrangement. She wouldn't even look at the baby. Whenever she did, it looked even stranger to her. She was probably tripping, but she couldn't shake the uncomfortable feeling.

Daddy ended his call. "That settles it."

Erica frowned at him with expectant eyes.

"You got your wish. Somebody's coming to get it."

Her heart skipped. She was afraid to be happy. She probably shouldn't be. After all, she was giving up her child. Despite her relief, she still wanted to know more. "Really? Who?"

As if on cue, Aunt Angie stomped into the room with quick steps. Erica turned to see her and inhaled a large gulp of air. Her wide gait didn't seem to slow her down as she reached for the child. "My goodness. Hey there."

It responded with a whine before starting to cry. Aunt Angie shushed the crying baby, bouncing it in her arms. Erica shook her head to stop herself from staring at the older woman.

"Your aunt is going to take it off our hands. You get to be a free woman now," Daddy said. Then he pointed at Erica. "But don't let that go to your head. You hear me? I better not get another one of these before you're married off or there'll be serious consequences." He gave her a stern look. Instead of it scaring her, it angered her. He didn't trust or believe in her. She wasn't Daddy's little girl—not that she'd ever been, but this wedge between them was a divide bigger than they'd ever had.

"I'm not gonna do this again."

"You'd better not," he reinforced.

Erica turned to leave. She couldn't hold in her anger any longer. She was tired of him giving her a hard time. Hadn't she been through enough? None of it was her fault.

Before Erica could exit, Aunt Angie reached out her chubby hand and grabbed Erica's arm. "Don't worry. I'll take good care of her."

Erica shrugged herself out of her aunt's hold and excused herself from the room. Her legs couldn't carry her fast enough. She needed to find the closest bathroom so she could throw up. She locked herself in the bathroom downstairs to get her bearings. After gagging a few times, she was able to slow her breathing. The warm lighting and marble countertop calmed her. She splashed cold water on her face and sat on the vanity stool, turning on the TV mounted to the wall. It seemed to take her attention off her troubles.

After watching a couple of shows, it was time to put this situation behind her. There was nothing she could do about her past. What was done was done, and her father would have to learn to forgive her—not for something that wasn't her fault but for not being the daughter he hoped for.

By nightfall, she concluded that the only way to get rid of these toxic feelings was to go out and join the world again. So she swallowed her disgust and got ready to go clubbing. Erica walked into the suite that she called her closet. On the wall were rows of folded clothing. Two rows were in the middle. Right where she stored her purses. Many of her color-coordinated shoes were kept in a glass cabinet for her to walk by and view. She snatched up outfits and tried them.

She settled on a gray, suede dress that hugged her curves. A glimpse of her new cleavage showed through an opening that went down to her stomach. As she pulled her hair together and piled it on her head, she secured it with pins, leaving it slightly tousled and framing her long face. The more layers of makeup she applied, the more she buried her problems. She topped it off with the brightest lipstick she could find and pouted in the mirror. That should do it.

About an hour later, she entered Hidden Jewel, an upscale, cool club, and immediately scanned the crowd. No one stood out to her yet. She moved to the bar and slammed back a few drinks. Each drink helped keep her problems from floating to the surface. Pretty soon, she was out on the dance floor, moving like no one was watching. She pretended she was on camera performing on a music video. She was the star. Suddenly she felt someone dancing behind her. She turned to see a man who looked like he was in his late twenties. He had a slight stubble and wore gray slacks with a red shirt. Erica figured he must be a banker or something. Even though he wasn't terribly neat, he certainly didn't look like a bum. His watch and swagger reminded her of money, and if there was one thing she knew, it was money.

Erica smirked at him and danced closer. He wrapped his arms around her waist, as they swayed with the music. She didn't ask his name, and she really didn't want to know. It wasn't like she would know him longer than the night. She could tell he thought the same because he didn't ask her name either. They grinded on each other for a couple songs without saying a word. Their bodies did all the talking.

Once they'd worked up a sweat, the banker led her off the dance floor and into the front area where a narrow hall was to their right. He led her away from the noise of the music, DJ, and crowd. They stopped midway, and he leaned her against the wall, kissing her gently. His lips were thick, and they tasted salty. Erica was curious about him.

When he leaned forward for another kiss, she latched onto his bottom lip and sucked it, tugging it away from his face. She thought she heard a faint quiver. He liked it. She smiled. What else was he about? As they kissed deeper, she ran her fingers up the back of his neck, running them through his hair. He grabbed her and pulled her closer to him. She felt so desirable and wanted. It was intoxicating. Euphoric. She was going to get lucky.

Chapter 2

Rendezvous Interrupted

Since she'd had several drinks, Erica was glad she hadn't driven to the club. She and the banker hopped in an Uber. They still hadn't said much to each other. Instead, the two held hands, giggled, and looked out the window occasionally. Erica's eyes wandered the scenery. Unfortunately, it made her mind wonder. It landed in the lowest part of her psyche. The part that wanted to make her feel bad about herself for all she was doing. And not doing. What kind of woman would go out drinking after she's had such a traumatic experience? One who was trying to move on with her life. Erica was tired of feeling sorry for herself. She was allowed to move forward. With that thought, she faced the banker and kissed him hard. He met her lips with the same force and passion.

The Uber driver pulled up to the black, iron gate at the Mercy mansion. The banker looked out the window and around the property. She was used to that. He didn't expect to be brought to such a place. Erica ignored his surprise and led him out of the car.

She didn't want to use the code to get passed the gate because the system kept a record of who came in and out. She also didn't want to alert her father that she was home because he would come looking for her. She hiked up her dress and climbed over the gate like she had many times over the last several years. The banker followed suit. They tiptoed over the immaculate lawn toward the left side of the mansion, where a three-bedroom guesthouse was located. Earlier, Erica left the main house without the key to the guesthouse, but sometimes the door was left unlocked. It wasn't like anyone was going to burglarize it in these parts. Everybody in the wealthy neighborhood knew each other. Erica reached for the doorknob and turned. This time, no such luck. She went around the back of the guesthouse and tried that door. Same result. Erica's eyes darted to and fro.

Could there be something around there that she could use to jimmy the door open?

The banker pulled her arm and turned her to face him. He planted a kiss on her, deeper than the one she gave him in the Uber. She responded by throwing her right leg around him. He leaned her up against the wall behind the house. She could tell by the bulge in his pants that he was ready to go. There was no time to wait. She pulled at his belt buckle to loosen it while he maneuvered his hands up her dress. He smiled wide as he reached inside her thong. She returned his smile and kissed him. Once she unzipped his pants, she went searching in his underwear like a kid opening a present on Christmas morning. She wasn't disappointed. She gripped his member and started to massage it. He leaned his head back, groaning. Then he lifted her dress to her waist to ease his member into her. He slid in easily. She smiled. He rocked her back and forth while he sucked on her breasts. After a few minutes, he picked up his speed. Her mind was racing. An engine that finally found freedom on the open road. For the first time in months, she felt liberated from her problems. Erica needed this.

He turned her around and entered her from behind where he increased his speed. She held onto the wall as they moved back and forth with the impact of his thrusts. Erica closed her eyes as the banker tightened his grip on her waist. She was right about to climax when she thought she heard the sound of a gun cocking back. She opened her eyes and turned to the side. Her father stood poised with his rifle in hand.

Erica jumped. "Agh. Daddy."

The banker jumped and grabbed his pants. He started to shake. "Sir. I'm sorry." He continued to shake while he tried to button his pants. The banker kept missing the loop. Eventually, he just zipped it up and yanked his shirt over it. He raised his hands beside him. "Easy, sir. I'll leave."

"What are you doing here?" Byron asked.

What a stupid question, but knowing her father, he was probably waiting for the banker to be a smartass so he could shoot him.

"I was making sure she got home safe," the banker said.

Daddy made a couple of steps closer to them. "You think I'm stupid, boy?"

"No, sir."

"Get off my property before I put a new hole in your head." Byron kept the shotgun fixed on the banker.

"Yes, sir. I'm leaving." The banker kept his hands raised as he passed Byron. Once he passed him, he all but sprinted down the green, grassy hill, as if a tiger were chasing him.

Her father turned his angry gaze on Erica. "What did I say earlier?"

Erica remained silent. She knew better than to interrupt her dad while he was on his tirade. He needed the time to tell her how lousy she was. Erica decided to let him get it over with. She turned toward him, unfazed by his shotgun.

"When are you going to stop acting like a cheap hoe?"

Erica crossed her arms and refused to answer. There was no point exposing her feelings to him. Time had proven that it wouldn't make a difference.

"Is this what you want to do for the rest of your life?" Byron asked.

Erica looked away, still refusing to answer.

"You'd better answer me, girl. Turning your nose up. I don't know who you think you are."

"I'm sorry."

Daddy narrowed his eyebrows. "No, you're not."

He was right—she wasn't sorry. She felt like she was old enough to do what she wanted. It was his fault if he wanted to keep treating her like a child and taking his anger out on her. She couldn't change what happened. He would have to get over it the same way she needed to get over it.

"OK, then I'm not."

Byron lifted the rifle and aimed it at Erica. She didn't flinch. Maybe it was the alcohol in her system. Maybe she wondered if he would really pull the trigger. Either way, she stood looking down the barrel of her father's gun.

Chapter 3

You Have to Leave

Byron stared at his daughter, eye to eye. "I have half a mind to put you out of this so-called misery of yours. Walking around the house moping. Like your life is so horrible. I've given you everything. Probably more than you deserve, and how do you repay me? Shame. Embarrassment. I had to hide you from people to keep them from talking, and I still think people have figured it out."

Byron was tired of dealing with his daughter's emotions. She needed to stop making excuses and do something to make her life better. From the looks of it, she was lapsing into old behaviors and doing things that got her into the problem he'd just solved for her. He didn't know what else to do. He thought scaring her would work or at least wake her up.

"Who cares? No one but you. I'm an adult. I don't live according to other people's standards," Erica said.

He narrowed his eyes. "Oh. I see now. I really have done too much for you. Yeah, I haven't allowed you to struggle and fight enough." Byron knew what he had to do. He slowly dropped the gun to his side. "I'm not gonna let you off easy anymore. You should have to live with your consequences longer, since you want to be such a smartass. I'll let you figure this shit out for yourself. I'm going to give you two months to get yourself together and get out of my house. I don't want to hear no excuses. I want you gone." He turned and walked back to the main house.

Byron was no fool. His daughter was not prepared to be on her own. Erica didn't have anywhere to go or anyone to call. She never had a real job, and he doubted she would be able to take care of herself, but he was tired of her foolishness.

Something had to be done. He had to make that clear tonight.

When he walked into his and Veronica's bedroom, Byron was still frowning. He had purposely decorated it to look like royalty lived there. They slept in a gold canopy bed with brown bed setting. Tassels tied the off-white curtains to the bed posts. It usually made him feel good, but as Byron walked on the shiny, white floor, bypassing the balcony, the events of the night still played through his mind like a movie reel.

Veronica sat on the bed, removing her earrings. She stopped when she saw her husband with his gun.

"What's going on?"

"Erica was outside the guesthouse with some loser."

"So?"

"She was fucking him." The very words made him sick. How could this be his daughter?

Veronica frowned like she'd swallowed something sour. "Are you kidding?"

Byron put his rifle back in the closet without answering. He didn't want to talk about it. He was still too upset. He thought Erica's accident would have changed her, but it didn't seem to have any affect.

"Maybe she's mentally ill," Veronica said.

"Nothing's wrong with her mental. She's just stupid."

"Hard to fix stupid."

"But you can make it stand on its own two feet," Byron said.

"What are you saying?"

"I've given her two months to get out of here."

"Really?" Veronica placed her hand over her mouth. It was too late. Her reaction didn't fool him. She was happy.

It was obvious that she and Erica didn't get along. They never bonded as stepmother and stepdaughter. He caught their biting comments toward each other. Erica expressed that she would never see Veronica as her mother. Veronica didn't help matters. She wasn't a mother. She didn't have a nurturing instinct. *She* didn't even have a mother. Veronica was a former model, and not a successful one—a fact she used to complain about, but now she appeared content to let Byron foot the bill for her comfortable lifestyle.

It puzzled him that both women knew what it was like to grow up without a mother's love, yet they felt no pull to connect. Byron had tried to get Erica and Veronica to talk. He later realized it was futile. The two women would always be on two different sides of the spectrum. Therefore Veronica's excitement didn't surprise him.

"I mean, if that's what you think is best," Veronica said.

Byron shot her a knowing expression. "Cut the bull."

She hesitated. "OK. So I think it's a good idea that she move out. She's been here too long. It's time for her to grow up."

He grunted in response.

"What's wrong?" She leaned over to put her arms around his neck.

"You know y'all don't like each other."

"That's a strong way of putting it. I think she could use a psychiatrist or something."

"You think my daughter is crazy?" He'd be lying if he didn't admit that this had crossed his mind. Her behavior was beyond unacceptable and no amount of punishment ever had an effect. He stopped short of recommending her to a shrink. What would people say?

"She could use someone to talk to," Veronica said.

"She could call her friends for that."

"Does she even have any?"

"She must." He wasn't sure. It had been awhile since he'd seen her with a friend. Byron couldn't say what had happened to them.

"A therapist would be better anyway. More objective."

Byron felt tightness in his chest. He grabbed it. "Sounds like an excuse to spend money to me."

"Are you OK?" Veronica stared at his hand.

He felt a slight pain in his chest. She helped him lay back on the bed. "Here. Take it easy. We can't have you getting all worked up over this. You're gonna need your strength this week."

Byron lay down on the bed and tried to steady his breathing. He closed his eyes to focus. Suddenly the pain went away. His anger about Erica went with it, temporarily. He was not happy about what she did, but he was glad he put his foot down. He was even more convinced that the ultimatum was a good idea. He could concentrate on other things now, like his annual party.

His parties brought all the who's who to Westbrook. It was important for his social circle. People liked to do business with someone they liked and trusted. This party was his way of staying front of mind and keeping his ear to the ground for opportunities. He was thinking about trying something new, like artist management. He would even consider real estate deals. He needed to network. Erica's issues would have to wait.

***

Byron was feeling much better the next morning. Or at least his chest was. Hopefully, it stayed that way. He refused to go to the doctor. The last time he was there the doctor tried to stick his finger up Byron's butt. That wasn't happening. People would do anything to you, if you let them.

He shouldn't have allowed that last thought. It led him back to his daughter. He preferred not to think about her troubles too long because it made him wonder where he went wrong and what he could have done to make her life better. Yet he kept coming back to the same answer. Nothing. There was nothing he could have done to save her from who she had become. Not even boarding school, in his opinion.

Byron leaned his head back on the sofa and closed his eyes. He hadn't slept much. His cell interrupted him before he could start snoring good. It was Shaun Lee, his old session drummer. He was also nephew of label head, Matthew Glover. For that reason, most people treated him delicately. He could be a real nuisance.

"I hear you have a party going on again this year," Shaun said.

"Yeah, I do," Byron answered, wondering where he got the information. He hadn't talked to the drummer in a while and for good reason. Word had gotten back to him that he was going around the industry bragging about his relationship with Erica. A big no-no. Erica was no angel, but Byron didn't tolerate the messy shit. He reached out to Matthew to get him to pull his nephew in, but from there he kept the boy at a distance.

"So what's up? I didn't get an invitation."

I don't owe you anything. "Oh, really?" Byron asked.

"I figured it must have been an oversight, right?" Shaun asked.

"You know, I think my guest list is full already. Maybe next year."

"Aww. That sucks . . . Hey, this isn't about Erica—"

"Listen, I gotta go. Talk to you soon."

Byron hung up before the young man could argue. He couldn't shake the conversation. He went looking for Veronica. He found her in the pantry area talking to Lana. He nodded down the hall. "Would you excuse us for a second?"

Lana dutifully scurried away.

"You're done with the guest list, right?" he asked Veronica.

"Sure. Why?"

"I got a call from Shaun Lee." He waited for recognition. There was none.

"I don't believe he's on my list. Did you want me to add him?"

"No . . . You're certain you didn't add him?"

She shook her head. "Did he say that I had?"

"No." Byron rubbed his hand over his wife's arm. She didn't know anything. No use burdening her with the details. "Don't worry about it. I handled him."

She smiled. "Did you want something for breakfast?"

He forced a smile. Veronica was not a good cook, and she knew this. Sometimes it seemed like she was testing him to see if he would tell her the truth. "I'll grab whatever I see." He headed toward the kitchen to grab a piece of the cake Erica baked.

Chapter 4

I Meant What I Said

As usual, Erica couldn't sleep. Not only were the nightmares bothering her, she now had a new concern: finding a place to go in two months. A big part of her didn't believe that her daddy would throw her out on the streets. She was still offended that he'd said it. She would address that with him this morning.

She decided to sneak downstairs to look for him in his office, but he wasn't there. She refused to go to his bedroom and risk running into Veronica. She went into the kitchen for some breakfast, figuring he'd make his way down by the time she was finished. It was around 8:30 in the morning. Maybe if she made him some French toast, he would navigate into the kitchen from the smell. He always liked her breakfasts.

Erica pulled out the necessary ingredients. While she was mixing everything together, Veronica trotted downstairs. Erica frowned at the sound of her steps. Veronica, a tall, slender woman who carried herself as if she were still a model, looked more like Cruella to Erica. Her sharp eyebrows and deep-red lipstick didn't help her stern looks. She really lucked out when she married Erica's father. She was married to an older man with money. That's all. There was nothing special about her. Erica found it ironic that her father liked to harp on her for not going to college and "making something of herself" when his own wife was a loser. Veronica wasn't the person Erica wanted to see early that morning, so she focused on dipping the bread in the egg mixture and putting it into the frying pan.

Veronica started in on Erica right away. "I'm surprised to see you up so early, given the night you had." The woman wore jean leggings and a dark-gray, long-sleeved blouse that hung off one shoulder.

Erica bit her tongue to keep from responding. She turned her bread over.

"That was quite a show you put on, but then again, how can I expect anything else from you?"

She hadn't even been there. How could she talk to Erica about what she did? Erica pulled two golden brown pieces of toast out of the frying pan. Veronica leaned on the kitchen island, clasping her hands together.

"What's your plan?" Veronica asked.

Erica frowned. "For what?" she mumbled.

"Where are you moving, since you know you can't stay here?"

She couldn't believe her father had told Veronica. "What does that have to do with you?" Erica asked.

"You're in my house."

Erica glared at Veronica. "Correction. This is my father's house."

"And your father and I are married, whether you like it or not."

"I'll stay here as long as I see fit."

Veronica smirked. "No, you won't."

"Who's gonna make me leave?"

"I will."

"I would love to see you try." She would knock the shit out of Veronica if she tried to force her out of her home.

"You'll be disappointed. It's not gonna go the way you think."

"I'm not going anywhere." Erica placed two more pieces of bread in the frying pan.

"We'll see if your father agrees when he finds out about the rumors that you slept with his drummer are true."

Erica walked around to the other end of the island to face Veronica. Pointing at her, she said, "You better watch your mouth."

Veronica narrowed her eyes. "I'm not scared of you no matter how tough you think you are. If you hit me, I'll get you put out today. No questions asked. It's not my fault you have more bones than a cemetery."

Cruella had no right to speak on things she didn't know. Erica was well aware of the music industry rumor mill. Many times that was all that it was—rumors. This particular rumor hurt more than any other because it was misrepresented. Yes, Shaun did have sex with Erica, but it wasn't consensual. It happened when she was fourteen years old, and he had caught her in the studio alone. She'd gotten out of school early and was looking for her father, who had left the studio to take a late lunch meeting with an executive.

Shaun seemed nice at first. He offered her a seat and something to drink—nonalcoholic, of course. She thought he was a good guy who was looking out for his boss's daughter while he was away. Erica learned different when he turned out the lights, pushed her on the couch, and covered her mouth. He told her that if she ever said a word he would tell everyone she came on to him. Shaun suggested that her father would be the laughing stock of the industry when everyone found out that his daughter was a whore.

When Erica finally caught up with her father that day, she didn't tell him, even though he asked her if something was wrong. Her father was very protective and serious about his business. Erica didn't want to draw any attention to herself and embarrass him. Even though she kept her mouth shut, she still became a part of the rumor mill. Some of it warranted—some not. She saw the disappointment in her father's face. She figured the best way to make him even angrier with her was to draw a map to the men she messed with. He would no doubt hear some familiar names, but Shaun was a different case. One that she had tried hard to forget. She wondered how in the world Veronica found out. She would not ask her.

"You're jealous, and my daddy will see straight through it. He will not believe your lies."

"I'm not lying, and you know it."

Erica's nostrils flared. "I know one thing. Let me find out you told my daddy some bullshit. I'll crack your head open." She moved back over to the stove and flipped the bread in the pan just in time. Veronica had some nerve trying to tell her that she was going to put her out. It was a shame that she still didn't know who she was dealing with, and if she tried her, she would find out very soon.

Even though she was still mad and frustrated, she managed to finish the French toast before stalking down the hall. Erica stopped short when she heard paper rustling. The noise was coming from the living room. She peaked in and saw her father on the couch, reading a newspaper. She tipped toed in.

The soft-orange walls and columns gave it an old look. Three large paintings lined the wall: one of the ocean, another of Italy, and the other of angels. She noticed that her father only had personal pictures in designated areas in the house where there were no visitors. She once asked him why he never put any personal pictures or paintings on the walls so people could see, and he said it wasn't "professional or their business." It was like him to think of his home as a professional place. It was for show and not for play or living. Erica picked at one of the flowers in the vase on the coffee table. This sparked her father to turn from his paper and look at her.

She flopped down next to him. "I made breakfast."

He grunted.

She looked at him. "Why don't you read Facebook?"

"Why the hell would I do that?" he asked without missing a beat.

"It's faster, easier."

"I do quite well with the paper."

"Too old school."

He stared at her. "Like I said. I do fine with the paper." Daddy returned his attention back to his paper and turned the page.

If Erica broached the topic of their fight last night, they might argue again. And she would get nowhere. So she tried to think of something pleasant to say. When she hadn't said anything yet, her father glanced her way again.

"What do you want?"

"Really? That's all you can say?"

"Don't play with me, little girl."

"That's negative."

He scowled at her.

OK, maybe I'd better get to the point.

"I'm still upset."

He turned the page in his paper.

Her skin turned hot. "What you said hurt me."

"What did I say?" Daddy asked calmly.

"You told me I was a hoe and I have to get out in two months."

"And this was after I caught you getting poked by some random idiot."

"That's not the point," Erica raised her voice. "I have a right to be here."

"Do you?"

"Yes, I'm your daughter. This is my home."

He turned the page on his paper.

Erica was getting annoyed with his dismissal. "OK. Then when are you gonna give me my money?"

"Excuse me? What money do you have?"

"The money you're gonna give me."

"How do you know I'm gonna give you anything?"

"You know you are." Erica crossed her arms. "If I have to move, I can't move with nothing."

"Get a job."

"You know I can't do anything." She didn't go to college. She hadn't even had a job before. This was unfair.

"I can let you work for me."

Erica couldn't imagine her father having another reason to order her around. "Never."

"Then good luck. The world is not free. By taking care of you, I've given you the false impression that someone would always foot the bill. Not anymore."

He hadn't been this tough with her before. There had to be only one reason why. "It's Veronica, isn't it? She has it out for me, and she told you to do this."

"No, and I'm not getting in the middle of that. Y'all need to work that out for yourselves."

Daddy could play this game, but he would never leave her destitute, homeless, and without resources. If he were that kind of father, he would have done that a long time ago. "C'mon, Daddy."

"No. I'm done talking about this." He got up from his seat and threw his newspaper on the coffee table. Erica watched him walk away. If he only knew that she was on the verge of hurting his wife.

Chapter 5

Money

No matter what Erica said, Byron was going to stick to his ultimatum. As a matter of fact, her attitude confirmed that he was making the right decision. She was spoiled. She needed to learn a lesson. After their discussion, he went to the back of the house to practice his swing. He wasn't good at golf. He only wanted to prepare for his meeting with some city officials. He looked forward to finding out more about the big wigs. Truth be told, he was getting bored and restless. Perhaps he could find a business to invest in. It would probably be entertainment-related. He missed the music industry, even though he wasn't motivated to go through his messages and review the eager artists who were looking for representation. He would have to do something soon or he would go stir-crazy.

The sun had peeked over the trees. It was starting to warm up. He could even hear birds chirping. This was his favorite time of day. His cell rang in mid swing. He stopped and reached for it in his back pocket. It was his sister's number.

"What's wrong?" he asked.

"This girl is really sick."

"Huh?"

"Megan."

"Who?"

"Oh, that's what I named her."

He shook his head. "Why are you calling to tell me this?"

"I know you don't care about her."

"What do you want?" Byron snapped. He didn't want to hear any lectures on how he should feel about this situation. It had caused a lot of issues in his house, and he gave the kid to his sister because she asked to keep it, as opposed to seeing it in foster care. Personally, he thought adopting it out would've been better.

"Money."

"For what?"

"Do you have butter in your ears? I told you. This baby is sick."

He might have asked from what, but he really didn't care. He only wanted it handled. "How much do you need?"

"The pediatrician is sending her to a specialist . . . I think $1,500 would cover it."

That was a lot of money. "What else?"

"I can't put her on my insurance yet, and these bills are no joke. Do you want me to send them to you?"

"No." He rubbed his eyes. Veronica came sauntering out. She placed a gentle kiss on Byron's lips and sat on the patio furniture. "I'll deposit it into your account tomorrow." Byron hung up the phone.

"Who was that?"

"My sister."

"Oh. How is she?"

"She wants money." He swung the golf club.

"Don't we all. You know your daughter hates me."

He sighed. "I really don't feel like hearing this right now."

"Of course not. You've been avoiding it for the last seven years."

"Then why are you bringing it up now?"

"Because she's rude."

There was nothing Byron could do about the fact that Erica didn't like Veronica. He wished she could get over that. He gave up a long time ago. He scrutinized his green lawn before swinging. "She'll always be rude."

Veronica paused. "I've been thinking about IVF. I heard a lot of people have success with it."

Byron squinted. "What's that?"

"Treatment for infertility."

"Um hm." Byron didn't feel like going down this road again either. Why couldn't she face the fact that she couldn't have kids?

"Do you want to go on an appointment with me?"

"I'm gonna be very busy. You know the party is tomorrow. I don't want to get distracted."

"It'll be after then."

"We'll see."

"But this is about family."

"I understand that . . . you can go and tell me about it. OK?"

"Don't you want another child?"

No, yet that wasn't what she wanted to hear. She'd been talking about babies nonstop, especially after she found out she'd had difficulties reproducing. He'd tried straight talk. It didn't seem to make any difference. "It's up to you. I can go either way."

Byron swung his golf club again, hoping that would be the end of the discussion, and it was for the time being.

***

It was party time, and everyone in the house was so involved in getting things right that there wasn't time to do anything else. Hired help hustled and bustled to get the food ready. Byron stayed on them. He was using the same company he often used. They knew his expectations. Everything had to be perfect or it would have to be redone. Of course as they neared time for the party, this was more difficult to accomplish.

"You're doing that wrong. Can't you see that?" Byron shouted at a pastry helper whose sweets were looking lopsided.

Veronica came running. She put her hand on his back. "Why don't you let me handle this?" She led him away from the helper, who stared after them with wide eyes.

"The guests will start arriving in forty minutes. They have to get it right."

"Go relax for a few minutes." Veronica pushed him toward the living room.

By the time the guests started to arrive, he was in better spirits. He was in his element, schmoozing the guests like a pro.

"Hey!"

Byron turned to see Rodney Parks, an old studio engineer friend. They worked on various projects together for chart-topping artists. He was happy to see him. They hadn't seen each other in almost a year. The two men bear-hugged.

"You picking up weight, huh?" Byron said.

Rodney touched his protruding gut. "Everybody can't have a fast metabolism."

They chuckled. "That's alright. You look good, man. How's the business?"

"You know people come and people go. I'm still here."

"That's right."

"You should be here too."

Byron shook his head. He played it down, even though he was itching to move forward. While he missed music, he had to be sure that his next opportunity was on point. The industry had changed so much. He couldn't keep up with the nonsense artists were spitting these days. It was so messed up that his last few productions were flops. The failure hurt a lot more than he let on. It made him step back and regroup before he started to doubt himself.

"Not right now."

"C'mon. You mean to tell me you don't tinker down there in your studio from time to time? I know you do."

"How do you know I have a studio?"

"Nobody gives it up completely."

He was right. Byron had created a studio in the basement. "I didn't say I don't still mix stuff and listen to it in my spare time, no matter how rare that time may be, but even if I do, I still don't have plans to return to the industry right now."

"I'll never believe it, man. It's in your blood. As a matter of fact, Leon didn't believe it either."

Byron flinched. He wasn't sure if his reaction betrayed him. After watching Rodney wave the young man over, he figured it didn't. Leon dutifully walked to where the two men were standing, a smile on his face. Byron wanted to wipe it off. Leon clearly didn't realize the truth about their hidden father-son scandal.

It was only a one-night stand, but it was enough for Leon's mother, Tiffany, to claim that Byron was his father. Erica's mother had left shortly after the accusation, even though he denied the little boy. It still bothered Byron that he had caused so much chaos in his life. He didn't want to believe Leon was his offspring and chose not to claim him. His anger rose to a feverish pitch when the youngster showed up in the music industry to work with him eighteen years later. It was almost like Leon was there to taunt him. Byron did not want this boy in his house.

"What's going on?" Leon asked.

"Nothing." Byron shoved his hands in his pockets.

"Great party. I didn't know you lived up here now," Leon said.

"Yeah. Would you excuse us for a minute?" Byron held up one finger and pulled Rodney to the side. Rodney followed his lead and listened closely as they moved out of earshot.

"Why did you bring him over here?" Byron asked.

"What?"

"I didn't ask you to bring him."

"Oh, c'mon. You don't still have an issue with him, do you?"

Byron pressed his lips tight together.

"Why don't you guys talk?"

"I don't have nothing to talk about." Byron didn't want to talk to this guy. As a matter of fact, he was already tired of talking *about* him.

"Whoa. Calm down."

"I'm calm. Just ... take him out of here, OK?"

Rodney patted him on the back. "OK. Don't worry about it. I got it. I'll call you."

He walked off, and Byron breathed a small sigh of relief. He would feel much better when he was gone.

Byron was relieved when he found an old friend to take his mind off seeing Leon at his party. "How you been Omar?" Byron asked. Omar Woods worked with him on a couple of charities. He had a good heart and a love for the ladies. Overall, he was a good man to know.

"It's been good. I have a few new hires I wanted you to meet. They couldn't come. I did bring my nephew here, though." Omar looked around the growing crowd. He spotted him from a far and waved. "Alonzo!"

A man that looked in his late twenties, six feet with a neat mustache and custom-tailored designer suit, nodded and headed in their direction. Byron sized him up as he walked over to them.

"This is my nephew, Alonzo Slade."

Byron shook hands with Alonzo. The young man's grip was firm. So far, so good.

"Honored to meet you, sir. My uncle has told me so much about you," Alonzo said.

"Please call me Byron."

Alonzo nodded. "Sure."

"Are you from here?" Byron asked.

"No, I'm from North Carolina."

"What made you come here?"

"I want to start fresh."

"What are you trying to start?"

"I want to manage artists. I also dabble in other things too."

"Like?"

"Trading."

Byron raised his eyebrows. "You don't say?"

Alonzo nodded.

"I've tried having him work with me, but . . ." Omar said, shrugging.

"I appreciate my uncle's help. However, I'm really fascinated with music. That's where the inspiration is," Alonzo said. "That's where the world changes."

"Is that so?" Byron asked.

"Yes. Music makes people do all kinds of things, bad and good. It's powerful."

Byron was impressed with the man. A bit of a dreamer, yet he appreciated that Alonzo wasn't like other young men his age. They just wanted to have fun. He'd hired a few of those to teach them the business and quickly had to get rid of them. Alonzo seemed set on his future. Byron looked at his hand and noticed there was no wedding ring. He thought of Erica. If he could find her, this would be a good time to introduce them. Even if he couldn't, he didn't want to lose touch with the young man.

"You know, I can help you with that. Take my number. Call and schedule an appointment tomorrow," Byron said.

Alonzo smiled wide. "Thank you, sir—I mean, Byron. I appreciate that."

After exchanging numbers, Alonzo moved on to meet more guests with Omar.

Another hour passed with music and drinks still flowing. People laughed and socialized as usual. Despite some minor hiccups, the party was another success. Byron couldn't help but notice that he hadn't seen his daughter in a while. He decided to go searching for her. He never knew where she would end up. After looking around the first floor, he ventured up the second floor and checked a few rooms until he saw movement on the balcony. He found Erica talking to Leon with a drink in her hand.

Chapter 6

New Man

Erica's soft laughter changed when she saw Daddy approach, nostrils flared, and she braced herself.

"What are you doing?" he barked as he stalked toward them.

"I'm having fun. Is that OK?" Erica frowned. Daddy grabbed her and pulled her away from the railing. "Daddy, I didn't do anything wrong."

"Daddy?" Leon asked.

"I want you out of my house," Daddy said to him.

"I ran into Erica and we sparked a conversation. She's very nice," Leon said.

Daddy leaned over Leon. "I'm not gonna tell you again. Get out." He pushed him.

Leon was slow to move, and Daddy pushed him a second time. "Go."

"You don't have to go anywhere." Erica couldn't believe her father was acting this way.

Leon edged toward the door. "It's OK. I'll see you later."

"No, you won't," Daddy said.

Erica huffed. "What did you do that for? Are you happy now?"

"I don't know what your problem is, but you need to get over it. Time to grow up."

"I am grown. In case you haven't noticed, I'm a woman now."

"Is that why you're messing around with any idiot who comes your way?"

"We didn't do anything." She saw he didn't believe her.

"Doesn't mean you weren't planning to."

"What difference does it make? You can't control me." Erica stomped off.

"I can't wait to you move out of here."

Those words cut through her to the core. What was she doing that was so wrong? Nothing but living her life. She was not his property. At this point, she wanted to leave. Where would she go? The fact still remained that she didn't have any money. Her dad had all the money, and he was holding it hostage, telling her to get a job. He probably wanted her to go to college and get a Series 7 license or something. None of which was interesting to her. She wanted to travel more. See the world. Not be hogtied to a desk or computer. He didn't understand that. He also didn't understand the type of men she liked. She didn't want a bookworm—she wanted a real man. Somebody she could relate to. It would have been great if she already had one. She could've moved in with him.

Erica found herself back downstairs, looking for another drink. She caught one from a waiter walking by and stopped to down it. The bubbly felt good circulating through her body, helping her forget about her problems with her father and his constant disapproval. The alcohol gave her some perspective.

Maybe she could find a way to get her father's money. Perhaps it didn't have to be his money at all. Her heart lifted at her train of thought until she saw Veronica approaching with a nightmare in tow.

"Erica, remember Shaun Lee?" she said. Then she turned to him and beamed. "So glad you could make it."

Shaun gave Erica a knowing but polite smile. "Hey," he said while he scanned her body with an unholy lust. Erica seethed and started to shake. The more she tried to still herself, the worse it seemed to get. She felt like she was about to black out. How dare Veronica do this to her at Daddy's party?

Before she knew it, Erica grabbed some food on a nearby tray and threw it at them. No matter what, Erica would not let Cruella intimidate her. Nearby guests scrambled to dodge the flying food. Veronica and Shaun ducked. Erica threw whatever she could get her hands on—spoons, forks, candles—at her offenders. She lost track of how long she'd been throwing things at them. She felt people grabbing her from behind, and her father grabbed her face.

"Stop it. Now!" her daddy shouted.

It took about a minute for her to focus on him. Everything was a blur. She heard her father say, "Take her to my office," and a couple of guests dragged her out of the party area.

Erica could hear Veronica shrieking, "She's crazy. Look at my dress."

The good Samaritans pulled her into her father's office and left her there. "You stay here and cool off," one of them said as they closed the door behind them. It was then that she started to feel her worst. She couldn't stand the phoniness and lies anymore. She had to find a way out of all this. It couldn't be her life. Everywhere she turned, her past greeted her. Reminded her of the mistakes and shame she carried. It was almost too much to bear. Tears started to stream her face. To stop them, she tried to find something in the room to focus on.

While people were still partying and gossiping about the scene she made, she slid behind her father's desk and turned on the small light. It illuminated just enough of the office for her to see, but not enough for the light to travel across the room.

She searched the drawers, first finding random papers and plans and then coming across bank statements. She reached farther into the drawer and found a small key stuck to the side. She pulled it off and looked around for a place that it would fit. After trying three key holes, she wiggled it into a small filing cabinet and pulled the drawer open. She found more information about safe deposit boxes and stocks. One financial statement showed $312,618 paid in royalties. She saw another document with Daddy's social security number and driver's license. Suddenly an idea hit her. She pulled her phone out of her cleavage and took a quick picture of his information before stuffing it back into the cabinet. This might be helpful.

***

Erica woke up, glad that the party was over. She was looking forward to today. She had a plan, and she was pretty confident it would work. She pulled on a high-waist, blue and white romper, matching it with silver bracelets. She then grabbed her iPhone before going downstairs to wait for Leon. To pass time, she walked out on the deck, sipping on a glass of orange juice.

"Great party last night." Veronica said, swishing by. Her gold bracelets jingled as she walked.

Erica tensed at the sound of her stepmother's voice. She made herself count to three. *One . . . two . . . three.*

Veronica started playing with her necklace. "You know that was a stupid stunt you pulled."

"Not nearly as stupid as the one you tried."

"I only brought an old friend by to say hi. You went all coo-coo for cocoa puffs."

"Both of you are lucky you're still standing."

"I know your luck is running out. Your father is not happy about your behavior."

"Did you tell him about yours?"

"I didn't do anything wrong. I was attacked by a wild animal," Veronica said.

Why did Erica even bother reasoning with her? No amount of logic would make sense to her.

"Your days here are numbered. It's OK. Maybe you can move in with your new boyfriend."

"Shut up."

"The guy you were talking to on the balcony. What was his name? Leon?" This clearly wasn't a real question. Veronica only wanted to continue to aggravate her.

"Whatever his name was, I don't know him," Erica said.

"OK. I thought I would help spark your memory so you can call him for a place to stay." Veronica grinned.

"While you're at it, try remembering the last time you were pregnant." Erica slapped herself on the forehead. "That's right. You can't get pregnant." On that note, Erica turned and left the deck with her glass of orange juice.

As Erica walked toward the other side of the house to get away from Veronica, she passed her father's office.

"Erica!" she heard him shout.

Aw, man. He was ready to chew her out for the scene she made last night. Erica searched her brain trying to figure out how to explain herself. Her father still didn't know what Shaun had done to her, and she couldn't fix her lips to explain it. He called her again, and she figured she'd better answer.

"Yes, Daddy."

"Come here."

She turned to walk into his office. As she walked down the steps, she saw him sitting with a man wearing a tailored, gray and white suit. She didn't think she'd seen him before, and she wondered why her father wanted her in their meeting.

"Alonzo, I want you to meet my daughter, Erica." He turned to Erica. "This is Alonzo Slade."

Erica glanced at him and nodded. "Hello."

Alonzo stood to greet Erica. "Good afternoon. OJ, eh?"

She shrugged. "What can I say? I like vitamin C."

"Me too. It's important. So is breakfast. It's not only the most important meal of the day. It's often the most fun too." He winked.

Was he flirting with her in front of her dad? That was weird. "I guess."

"We're meeting about some mentoring opportunities. We have a few minutes. Why don't you show him around?" Daddy asked.

Erica looked puzzled. "But I was about to—"

"It won't take long." He smiled. To the outside eye, it might look like a calm, friendly grin, but Erica knew what that grin meant, "Do this or else." Given that she had already made a mess of his party, she figured she'd better comply.

"Sure. Come this way," Erica put her glass down and headed toward the door. Alonzo followed behind her.

"What do you do?"

Erica turned and looked at him.

"I mean, where do you work?" Alonzo asked sheepishly.

"Who wants to know?"

"Me. I'm asking."

"Are you looking for employees?"

"No. Not yet. Your father is graciously putting me in contact with people who can help me get my foot in the door in music."

"Good for you," she said, allowing her response to be as dry as possible. What a turnoff. She didn't want to hear anything about music men.

"Do you like living in Florida?"

She frowned. "You ask a lot of questions."

Alonzo chuckled. "You're not asking any. Somebody has to break the ice."

"What do you want me to ask you?"

"Am I from here? Who's my family? Am I married?"

Erica knew he thought too much of himself. Why would she care if he's married or not? Had they been in a club, she would have brushed him off a long time ago, but since he was working with her father, it was a bad idea to treat him like a dirty, wet rag. She would no doubt hear about it later. "Is that what you want me to ask you?"

He shrugged.

They walked down the hall.

"Are you from here?" she finally asked, rolling her eyes.

"No, I'm from Carolina."

"Why did you come here?"

"I came down to be with family and see if I could make a career." He stopped short to read the music awards, plaques, and platinum records on the wall. "This is amazing."

"What was wrong with Carolina? I guess you couldn't make it there?"

"Not like I wanted." They started walking again. "Besides, I thought my uncle could help. So far, he has."

"How?"

"By putting me in the places where I can meet key people, like your dad. He really is a cool man."

"I suppose."

Alonzo raised an eyebrow. "You don't agree?"

She shrugged. "He's my father. I don't know him to be any different."

"I guess it's hard to see a parent for their accomplishments."

"I see what he does. It's just not that important to me."

"Then what is?"

It was a deep question she wasn't sure she should get into now. "Being free."

They turned the corner and ran into Veronica.

Chapter 7

Can You Help Me?

"Well, hello there," Veronica said. She swayed her drink back and forth, causing the ice in her glass to jingle. She shot Alonzo a crooked smile, which made Erica roll her eyes.

"Hello, ma'am," Alonzo nodded at Veronica.

"What's your name?" she asked.

"Alonzo Slade."

"Veronica Mercy. The lady of the house." She leaned forward and shook his hand. "Haven't I seen you before?"

"I was here for the party. It was great by the way. Thank you for your hospitality."

"Why, you are welcome. Despite unfortunate incidents, it was a pretty good night. Such a gentleman. I like that. Don't you?" Veronica looked at Erica.

Erica said through gritted teeth. "Yes, of course."

"I know it's so different from what you're used to. What a breath of fresh air."

Erica could have choked Veronica. Before she did, she decided to keep Alonzo moving.

"If you don't mind, I have to finish the tour. Daddy's request. That leaves you to go—" she allowed her voice to trail off as she gave Veronica a once over, "—do whatever you do."

Veronica sucked her teeth and turned her attention back to Alonzo. "I look forward to seeing you again. Don't be a stranger," she said, before walking away.

"I won't."

Alonzo and Erica rounded the corner. "That was awkward," he said.

"She's awkward."

"I take it you two aren't friends."

Erica felt a buzz in her pocket. She grabbed her phone and saw a text from Leon. He was outside. "Not even close," she said, distracted.

Her father rounded the corner, and she thanked God that the tour had come to an end. "There's my dad."

Alonzo leaned over and whispered in her ear as they approached her daddy. "You forgot to ask me if I'm married."

"Maybe next time," Erica said.

"How did it go?" Daddy asked.

"You have a lovely home," Alonzo said.

Daddy nodded. "Thank you, son. I have lunch set up for us." He turned to Erica. "You'll be joining."

"No."

"Yes."

"I have other things to do, Daddy. I'll see you later." When she leaned over to kiss him on the cheek, he grabbed her arm.

"I need to talk to you today," he whispered.

Even though his voice was low, Erica could hear the tension in it. She nodded and trotted out the door. At least she was able to dodge the tongue lashing for a few more hours. She had plans that would change everything, if she could just get out this door to talk to Leon without her father knowing that he was there.

Erica made it down the grassy hill and out the iron gate. Leon leaned on his car, a gray Honda Civic, waiting for her. She kissed him on the cheek and hugged him. He returned the strength of her hug.

"Thanks for coming," she said.

"I'm glad you reached out. I didn't know what to expect after your dad kicked me out." Leon hung his head.

"I'm sorry. You didn't deserve that. My father's really uptight these days. Mostly about me. Not about anything you did."

"I beg to differ. Your father never liked me much, even when I helped with engineering on his last couple of projects. I'm not sure why." Leon stared at the house with a faraway look in his eyes. Erica noticed a subtle longing in his boyish features.

As far as her father, there was no telling. He was funny sometimes and didn't like a lot of people. She didn't want their meeting to digress into a lengthy conversation about his proclivities. That would go on forever.

"Trust me. Don't sweat it."

He nodded. "So what did you want to talk to me about?"

"I have a favor to ask." Erica paused. She couldn't believe she was doing this. It seemed like a crazy idea, yet it might be off the wall enough to work. Besides, she couldn't think of anyone else to ask. "Would you mind if I use your address?"

"Huh? For what?"

"I need to complete a form, and I really don't want to use my address."

"Why not?"

"Because I want my dad out of my business."

"What is it you don't want him to know?"

Erica debated on telling him about her plan to open a credit card in her father's name without his permission. It wasn't like he would tell. Daddy didn't like him. She was certain he wouldn't stick around to hear him snitch on her. Then again, she wasn't 100 percent sure she trusted him either. She met him last night. Her father had known him for at least a few years, and *he* didn't even like him. Strangely, that might be a good way to keep her dad from finding out.

"I don't want him to pass judgement on me, OK? You don't know what it's like to have a father as stern as mine."

"I don't know. I'm iffy about giving my address to someone to use without understanding what's going on."

"Fine. I'm going to open a credit card."

"Wait. That's all?"

She nodded.

"And you can't use this address?"

"I don't wanna hear Daddy's mouth."

Leon raised his eyebrow. Erica could tell he thought her reasoning was suspect, but she didn't see the reason to explain everything to him. It was more important that she get what she wanted so she could have the money to move out in two months.

"What's in it for me?" He gave her a devilish grin.

Here we go. Somebody always had their hand out. She really wanted his help. She would have to give him something.

"What do you want?"

"How much is the card limit?"

"It's $25,000."

"I want 10 percent."

"To use your address?" This was crazy.

Leon stepped closer to her, cocked his head, and started to rub her back. "It's up to you."

Erica's stomach flipped. She had a bad feeling about this situation. It was more complicated than she expected. She thought this might be her best opportunity to get money quickly. Her days at home were numbered, and who knew what her father would do after the fight she had with Veronica and Shaun at the party?

She heard a car coming up the graveled driveway. She looked to see who it was but saw the car backing out and turning around.

"A flat $2,000 is all I can do."

"For you, I'll oblige. When you plan to do this?" he asked.

She sighed. "As soon as possible."

He said that was OK, and they said their goodbyes. She walked back to the house, frustrated. Erica wanted to believe that there was a better way to do this, but she didn't have anyone else with an address she could use. Maybe once she got on her feet she would be able to pay her father back. That thought made her feel better about using his information. This money would make a difference, and it would be worth it in the end.

Chapter 8

You Like Her

Once Byron and Alonzo finished lunch, they migrated to Byron's pool room, drinks in hand. The room was situated beside his office. The décor was cabin like with wooden walls. He wanted to make the atmosphere more comfortable because he wanted Alonzo to be open to his suggestion. It shouldn't be hard. What man wouldn't want a father's blessing to date his daughter? It didn't happen every day. He liked Alonzo. He was an ambitious, young man and that was always better than a bum. Plus, Byron saw the way he looked at Erica when she walked in the office. He knew that look. Alonzo would be relieved to hear that Byron was giving him the green light. He hoped the young man responded appropriately.

Byron put his drink down and reached for the pool sticks. "Do you play?" he asked Alonzo.

"Sure."

Byron handed him a stick.

Alonzo grabbed it and placed his drink on a nearby table. "How long have you lived out here?"

"About six years. When I bought the property, I added some things to make it more comfortable. I think it helped."

"I would say so. It's beautiful."

"Thank you. I may look into some real estate development eventually."

"There's a lot to work on around here but especially on the outskirts. Plenty of land waiting to be developed and people looking to expand. Maybe I can introduce you to some people."

Byron smiled. "I'd like that. I may take you up on your offer." This was a good sign. It showed that Alonzo wanted to impress him. There probably weren't too many people he could introduce him to that Byron couldn't reach himself. Still, it was nice that he wanted to help. Byron had him where he wanted him. He bent forward and focused in on the white ball, tuning out the rest of the world. He hit the ball with the end of the stick, watching the colored balls roam around the green table until they settled. He'd knocked the blue and red ball into the hole.

"Great shot," Alonzo said.

"Show me what you've got."

Alonzo struck the white ball, knocking the green ball into a hole.

"Not bad. So . . . where do you see yourself ten years from now?" Byron asked.

Alonzo cleared his throat. "Managing at least three artists. A few properties. Maybe married with a couple of kids."

Byron smiled wide and nodded. It was almost like Alonzo knew where he was going with this. It was too perfect. "That sounds like an excellent plan. Any young lady in mind?" Byron took a swig of his rum and coke.

"Not quite. It's hard out here." Alonzo chuckled.

"That's what I keep hearing. Where do you look?"

"Stores, conferences, clubs."

Byron frowned. "Clubs are for hookups. One-nighters." He leaned over to take his turn at the pool table. The white ball flew across the green and bounced off the sides.

"I agree. To be honest, it really doesn't matter where I go. No luck."

"What are you looking for?"

"Someone smart, elegant, well-spoken. No hood boogers."

The two men laughed.

"A woman who can hold her own and be my partner in crime."

Byron nodded. "What do you think about my daughter?"

Alonzo raised his eyebrows. A smile tugged at one corner of his mouth. "Uh, she seems like a great woman. Very smart, articulate."

"Did you ask her out today?"

"No, sir. I didn't."

"Why not?"

Alonzo laughed and ran his hand over his head.

"No need to be nervous, son. I'm only asking questions."

"Frankly, I don't think she was interested."

"Ah." Byron fanned the idea away. "You're a man. You know how to change that."

"Maybe. I don't like to push myself on women who are resistant."

"I wouldn't want you to, but resistance is a part of the dance. If she's resisting your advances, at least she's giving it thought. And if she's thinking about it, there's a chance of changing her perspective."

"I suppose." Alonzo shifted his weight. "What do you want me to do?"

"Do you like Erica?"

"Sure."

"Ask her out to dinner. You have my blessing." Byron took a swig.

"When?"

"Preferably soon." Byron didn't need any more instances of finding Erica outside being plowed by some stranger. He'd rather her date a nice fellow like Alonzo. He might have his own faults. However, Byron believed he could be a good catch for her. Whatever Alonzo was missing, he could mold him into what he needed to be—as a husband and a man. "What do you say?"

"I'll ask her the next time I see her."

Byron shook his head. "Here's her cell number. I want you to give her a call no later than tomorrow. Got it?"

"Yes, sir. I'll do it."

Byron offered his hand. Alonzo shook it heartily.

"It's your turn." Byron nodded at the table.

As Alonzo leaned over to take another shot at the white ball, Byron thought about talking to Erica to make sure she was more receptive to Alonzo. It was for her own good.

Chapter 9

I Don't Have to Like You

Erica leaned over the balcony on the second floor, scrolling through Facebook. It was an aimless activity, but she used it to get caught up on what was happening in the world. Her 1,400 "friends" kept her in the loop, even though she kept them from finding out about her unwanted baby. She felt something pierce through her stomach. Was it guilt?

It couldn't be. She did the best that she could. Giving the baby to her aunt was the best thing.

No, it wasn't. You know who they are.

Erica swallowed hard and gasped for air. Before she could totally lose it, her father approached her.

"What was last night about?" he asked.

She shrugged. Partially because she didn't know what to say—largely because she was still catching her breath.

"Don't give me that. You know better. Now, what was the problem?"

She swallowed again. It was getting easier to do so.

"Answer me." Her father's voice was stern. He meant business.

"Why did you invite Shaun after all the nasty rumors he spread about me?" Erica erupted.

"I didn't. He was never supposed to be here."

"Then how did he turn up?"

"I don't know." Daddy rubbed his face. He usually looked young for his age, but in that moment, his face was worn, almost drooping. She thought she saw the beginnings of lines across his forehead. "You should have let me handle it. Don't ever make a spectacle like that. You need to be above that kind of stuff."

Her father was probably right. She wished he understood how hard it was to resist attacking the people who were taunting her. She could only take so much. Erica stared over the balcony. Her father put his arm around her shoulder.

"It's going to always be us against the world. Family over everything."

She faced him. "Then why do I have to move?" She couldn't have created a better segue if she tried. He was showing her that she wasn't over everything. Tired of the contradiction, she wanted answers.

"Because I have to let you go sometime. Go. Grow. I would actually like to see you married with children. Living a much better life than you've been in for the last several months." He paused and opened his mouth twice before continuing. "What did you think of Alonzo?"

"Who?"

"Alonzo. The young man you met in the office."

She frowned. "What about him?"

"Seriously, Erica. Do you like him?"

"No!" *Where did he get that idea from?*

"Relax."

"Just because I've made some mistakes doesn't mean I want everybody."

"That's not why I asked." Daddy leaned over the balcony. "I think he's sweet on you."

"And?"

"While I'm sure you don't consider him your type, it's time you start opening your mind."

"Since when do you tell me who to date?"

"Since you don't know how to pick people to date."

"So I haven't made the best decisions. I should still be able to pick out my own man." Erica crossed her arms.

"Be nice to him. You may change your mind about him in the future."

"No, I won't."

"Yes, you will. You have to grow up some time." With that, Daddy walked away.

Those words lingered with Erica longer than she wanted. That night, she wandered absentmindedly through the house to shower and change clothes. She wanted to give herself another night on the town. Perhaps she was still trying to "heal" herself or maybe she wanted to prove her father wrong. Either way she was heading out. She sprayed on her favorite White Tea perfume. The scent made her smile for the first time all day. It may have even been longer than that since the last time she showed some teeth.

She tried thinking of the pros in her life. Earlier that day, she had completed the online application for the credit card and now she would wait. Maybe she could finagle Leon's percentage down. Either way, it would all work out if she followed her plan. Get the card. Use the money from it to get a place and some furnishings. She would have to figure out how she would keep the place after she got there.

Erica swept her hair back and admired her deep-purple dress. The thin fabric gathered at her knees. To top it off, it showed a generous portion of her back. She was pleased.

When she left the room, her purple and gold heels clicked as she walked down the hall. At the bottom of the stairs, she saw Alonzo. What was he still doing there? It had been several hours since she saw him with her father.

"Where are you going?" Alonzo asked.

"I don't believe it's any of your business. What are you doing here?"

"I just wrapped up with your father. Why haven't you been around all day?"

"I've been busy." Erica walked passed him to leave. Yes, her father told her to be nice to Alonzo. That was before he became pushy. She didn't like that.

"I can take you where you wanna go."

"I'm quite capable of getting there on my own. Thanks."

"You look like you're ready to party. If you drink, you can't drive home. I can take you and whatever dude you're going to see can drive you back. Unless he doesn't have a car." Alonzo chuckled.

What a jerk. "Is that all you got?"

Alonzo stopped. "Let me take you. I know you're not scared."

Erica didn't need him to drive her, but she could not resist someone insinuating she was afraid of something. Besides, she did intend to drink. Maybe it wasn't a bad idea. He wasn't stupid enough to harm her. Daddy would kill him, and she *was* supposed to be nice.

She told Alonzo where she wanted to go and followed him out the door. In his dark-blue Mercedes Benz, Erica kept the window down. It blew her soft ringlets and the flaps of her dress to and fro.

"What business do you have with my father?"

"Music contacts. I'm also linking him up with some real estate." He glanced at her. "You want in?"

"Please."

"You sure? I'm surprised you never tried to get something going in the music industry."

She sucked her teeth. "It's nothing special."

"Why? You don't like it or you don't like the people?"

"Both." There was nothing she wanted to do in music. Most of the people were slimy criminals anyway. She didn't feel the need to tell Alonzo that. He would find out soon enough.

"Whenever there's money on the line, people do the most. You know what I mean? And you don't have to be in music to see the worst of that either."

"Then why do music at all?" she asked.

"It's a dream. Don't you have dreams?"

"I guess."

"You must dream of something."

Well, she tried to be nice. Unfortunately, she was growing tired of him already. "What's the point of this conversation?"

"I'm being pleasant while I take you to your destination."

"Silence is pleasant too."

He smirked. "Why are you so mean?"

"Am I mean or are you sensitive?"

"I'm sensitive to people talking to me any kind of way."

"Then I apologize. I guess I get testy when people ask me a lot of questions."

"I'll slack up on them."

"That would be great." Erica looked out the window. It was really dark now and all she could see was the faint outline of trees as they rode by. She didn't want to think about her life because it was still shaky. Between getting pregnant, giving up her child and being pushed to move out, she was having a bad year. She didn't have time to dream—she had to figure out how to survive. He didn't need to know all of that.

After a few minutes of riding in silence, Alonzo broke it. "I'm sorry."

"No need to apologize."

"I should if you were offended in some way. I wasn't trying to be rude. I was only trying to get to know you. If that came off wrong, I really didn't mean it."

"It's fine. I may have overreacted."

Alonzo nodded. "So what are your plans tonight?"

"Gonna go drink and dance a little. Blow off some steam."

"I hear that. I like to go to a Jamaican spot about fifteen miles from here every once in a while. What kind of music do you like?"

"Mostly R&B."

"If you ever want to check out a new spot, let me know. We can go there. They also have great food." He looked at her. "Yes, I'm asking you out."

She frowned.

"Are you thinking about somebody else?" he said.

"No." Why couldn't he catch a hint?

"I mean, you're not married so, I don't think dinner and dancing would hurt. If he wants to keep you, it'll make him step his game up."

Erica could feel herself getting angry again. He was talking without knowing what he was talking about. Instead of giving it a rest, he kept talking.

"I'm not married," Alonzo said.

She sighed. "Why should I care?"

"I'm saying that to say that neither of us have a reason to be tied down."

"It doesn't matter. Can't you take a hint? I'm not interested in going out with you. Geez." Erica stared back out the window.

"What is it with you? You don't like it when a man is nice to you? I know—you like it when a man is cursing you out."

"Just because you're driving me somewhere doesn't mean I have to kiss your ass."

Alonzo pulled over and stopped the car.

"What are you doing?" she asked.

He got out of the car and walked behind it. He went to her side and opened the door.

Chapter 10

First Time

Erica's heart was almost beating out of her chest. She scanned the car really quick to see if she could spot a weapon.

Alonzo grabbed her arm. "Do you wanna get out?"

A sharp pain traveled up Erica's arm, and she snatched it back. "No. Let go of me."

"Then quit treating me like shit."

"I don't know what you're talking about."

"You do. Cut that shit out."

He gave her an intense stare that sent a wave of fear through her. He finally walked back to the driver's side. Erica closed the door, shaken and angry. What was his problem?

After Alonzo got in, he closed the door behind him and sat there. Erica could hear him breathing harder than he was before. He broke the silence again. "I apologize. That was inappropriate."

"You're damn right. Who the hell do you think you are? You have no right to treat me this way. Wait 'til I tell my daddy."

Alonzo gazed at her. Erica couldn't tell what he was thinking. Was he going to slap her? Push her out of the vehicle? Instead, he did the unexpected. Alonzo leaned over and kissed her. She pushed him away. He backed up for a second. Then he kissed her again. Erica pushed against him as he pressed his lips against hers hard. She squealed. He grabbed between her legs, which concerned her. She wasn't wearing any underwear, so he had instant access. But despite her muffled objections, she was quite wet. He began to move his finger around in a circular motion, easing it into the opening. When he rubbed his thumb against her clit, she could not resist him anymore. She opened her legs for him to get a better handle on her.

Alonzo responded by shoving his finger farther into her. She moaned. He eased it out and in, and she moaned. This time, when he kissed her, she returned it, equaling his voracity. Meeting him tongue for tongue. Erica loosened the strap on her dress and the thin fabric fell off her body. He barely waited for her to pull it off before reaching at her bare breasts. As soon as he could, he sucked on her hardened nipples. They both pulled the dress down. Alonzo adjusted his seat and Erica climbed on him with nothing on other than her high heels. She unbuckled his belt. He unzipped his pants. She hopped on him and rocked back and forth. She went slow at first. Then she sped up. Alonzo rubbed her breasts and continued to suck on them. He slowly moved his hands to her butt, guiding her where he wanted her to be. His grip was so tight that Erica was certain he would leave his handprint on her skin. She wasn't worried, though. She enjoyed the ride, the escape.

After a few minutes, Erica switched to face the steering wheel and sat on his lap. She maneuvered him inside of her and rocked with him. She closed her eyes as her proverbial itch was getting scratched. Alonzo rubbed between her legs while she rocked. The sensations made her head spin. She rocked until finally she climaxed. Alonzo held onto her until he was finished as well. Once their joy ride was over, Erica and Alonzo fixed their clothes.

Alonzo cranked the car. "I'm taking you somewhere," he said.

He proceeded to drive several miles out, down long abandoned roads.

"Where are you taking me?" she asked.

"You'll see."

"I'd rather know."

"You don't like surprises?"

"No."

Alonzo smirked. "You'll like this one."

Erica wasn't fond of being told what to do. It reminded her too much of her father. However, she appreciated not being able to push a man around. It was hard to respect such a man, and the fact that Alonzo stood up for himself made her consider him someone worth respecting.

She bit her lip and looked out the window. The winding road led to more green hills, and the air smelled like salt. They parked at the Horseshoe, a harbor that was shaped like its name, where boats lined the coast. Alonzo got out of the car and went to her side to open the door for her. They walked to an Azimut 55S. The only reason Erica knew the yacht is that she was with her father when he took a few friends on one to celebrate an associate's birthday.

Alonzo escorted her onto the boat, where she stepped onto the plush beige carpet. He went to the steering wheel and led them out into the water. Erica helped herself to the liquor in the bar. She fixed herself a drink and made him one too. They rode for about thirty minutes before stopping in the middle of the ocean. The boat drifted in dark silence. Alonzo sat next to her on the white sofa, grabbing his drink. He clinked it with hers. "Cheers."

He took one big gulp, while Erica looked at the sea. "Do you come out here a lot?" she asked.

"Every now and then. My uncle likes it out here more." He looked at Erica. "You've never been out here?"

"I haven't come often." Yachts didn't really do it for her. They were boring.

"I went fishing a couple of months ago. Caught some pretty good ones."

"Why did you bring me out here?" She hoped he didn't intend to talk to her about fish all night.

"I thought you could use it."

"Why?"

He shrugged. "You looked like you had a lot on your mind. Am I right?"

Erica smirked and stared back out at the sea.

"You don't know me, but we can get to know each other. I've been watching you since your dad's party."

That figured. He seemed like he'd been on the prowl for a while. "Oh, really."

"Yeah." He looked her up and down. "If you let me, I could make you happy."

She rolled her eyes. "That's so lame."

Alonzo frowned. "Why would you say that? You don't wanna be happy?"

"Get outta here with that. You were starting to seem like an OK guy. Now you're throwing out pickup lines."

"No. I only wanted to relay that you should take a chance on me."

Erica stared at the dusk sky. Stars were about to form. There wasn't much to look forward to. Not here in Westbrook. Just a bunch of stuck-ups who thought their money made them interesting. Maybe she should take the credit card money and leave town. At least then she wouldn't be constantly reminded of her problems. Erica wondered if her mother was thinking that when she left her. Suddenly her mood sank.

Alonzo moved closer and elbowed her. "Hey. What's wrong?"

Erica shook her head.

"C'mon. You can talk to me."

"I don't know what I'm gonna do with my life," she said.

"You're still young. You'll figure it out."

"I don't need to figure it out. I need money."

"Don't we all," he chuckled.

Erica didn't find a damn thing funny. As a matter of fact, his laughter annoyed her. He didn't understand her situation and probably never would. "Take me home."

"What?"

"I want to go home," Erica said more assertively.

"Why? I thought we were getting to know each other. Having fun."

"I didn't ask to come out here and I'm ready to go."

"Listen. If I've said something to offend you, I'm sorry. Really." He grabbed her hand. "Please. I don't want you to go."

Alonzo leaned closer to her and kissed her softly. She pulled away.

He grabbed her hand and led her to the back of the yacht, where there was a master suite. Brown and beige décor greeted them as Alonzo sat on the bed and pulled her closer to him. He wrapped his arms around her waist and looked at her. He moved his hands down, reaching under her dress to grip her butt.

Erica didn't know what she saw in Alonzo. He definitely wasn't her type, and she couldn't see herself with him long term. For now he seemed to be the thing that she needed. At least she didn't go to the club and bring anybody home. In a way, he was bringing her home. She leaned down and kissed him passionately.

Chapter 11

Denied

lonzo lifted her dress up as Erica climbed over him. They tongued each other before hers moved down his chin to his neck and his chest. She slipped her dress over her head and reached into his pants and began massaging his member. Unable to control himself, Alonzo rolled her over and pulled his clothes off. He entered her on top of the covers. Their bodies met each other stroke for stroke. He buried his head in her breasts.

They spent the rest of the night matching each other's energy and passion. By the time they finally fell asleep, it was late morning. When she awakened, the clock read 12:13 p.m. She did not mean to be with him that long. Erica could only imagine what her father or Veronica would have to say. She threw the covers off and slipped her dress back on.

Alonzo was already up front and smiled when he saw her. "Morning, sunshine. Do you want to go somewhere for brunch?"

She squinted at the light bouncing off the water and into the boat. "No. I'll be heading home now."

"Sure? I know a great spot. Quaint, private."

Erica took this as code for his house. She wasn't interested. He was a good lay, but right now she was in the mood for a bath and a nap. "No thanks."

This time, he dutifully cranked up the boat and steered it back to the harbor. They said very little to each other on the ride back to the Mercy mansion. She found herself wondering how their relationship would play out. It was awkward and risky to have a fling with someone her father was connected to professionally. Even though he gave her the go ahead, she was so used to hiding this part of her life from him. She didn't know what to expect from here.

"Thanks for the rides," she said after he stopped in front of the gate.

Alonzo laughed. "You're quite welcome. I look forward to giving you more. When can we make that possible?"

"We'll see."

"If you need anything, call me. I mean it."

Erica stored that information into her mental filing cabinet as she opened the car door and waved goodbye.

While she punched the code for the gate, Alonzo peeped his head out his window. "Don't make me wait too long."

Erica rolled her eyes and walked onto the property. She entered the house in time to catch Veronica primping in a nearby mirror. She was wearing a blue and white bathing suit that was cut out in the front and the sides. Erica wasn't looking forward to seeing her. Unfortunately, it was too late to go around the other side.

"Are you just getting in?"

"I don't know."

"Don't get smart with me."

"I would never do that. You wouldn't be able to keep up." Erica walked around her and down the hall. She reached in a drawer and snatched up her father's credit card.

"Why do you have to be such a bitch?" Veronica asked.

Erica stomped up the stairs. "Go cry somewhere about it." While she was waiting for her card to come, she would treat herself to a little spree.

***

After Erica took a shower and rested up, she was ready to spend some of her dad's money in retail therapy at her favorite store, Nordstrom. Her father would never suspect anything different because she always used his card for shopping. He generously and routinely supplied it without question. She spent a couple of hours plowing through the racks before finally hauling her clothes up to the counter. Yes, she would be buying all of these.

The sales girl rang it up while Erica pulled out her phone and checked her messages. Leon had texted her a few times that morning, wondering if everything was still a go. She texted back, *Yep, it's done. Will have ur $ shortly.*

Erica looked up and saw that the sales girl was ringing up the last of her items. She pulled out her daddy's card and waited for the opportunity to insert it.

"That will be $5,842.02," the sales girl quoted the price.

Erica inserted the card and waited for recognition. At first, there was nothing. Then there was movement on the little screen with an alert that the card was rejected. *What?* That couldn't be. The sales girl automatically cleared the message for her to try again. Erica swiped a second time and received the same message.

"This doesn't make any sense," Erica snapped. She was too angry to be embarrassed.

"Let me see it." The sales girl grabbed the card and punched the numbers into the cash register. She waited but returned a disappointing look. Obviously, it didn't go through. "Sorry."

"I don't know why this is happening. It's my dad's card. It always works. There must be something wrong with your machine."

"I'm afraid not."

"There's definitely something wrong. Daddy always has money on his cards."

"Well, he doesn't today." The sales girl started to laugh but caught herself when she saw the look on Erica's face.

"My father makes a lot of money. So you can wipe that funky smile off your face."

Erica hated that she felt the need to defend her father against stereotypes, but she didn't mind it in this scenario. No one would treat her or her father like they were some lowlife hoodlums. She pushed her purse over her shoulder and dashed out of the store. She tried calling her dad as she reached the car. He didn't answer. Probably stepped away from his phone. She kept trying as she drove straight home. She was never able to get him when she needed him.

Erica opened the front door and slammed it behind her.

Veronica yelled from around the corner. "What are you slamming that front door for? This isn't your house."

Geez, didn't she have something else better to do today. She was everywhere. "Shut up, Veronica."

Veronica marched into the foyer. "Watch your mouth."

"No, you watch yours. I don't have time for your foolishness right now."

"What's your problem?"

"Daddy's card doesn't work. Do you know anything about that?" Erica wouldn't be surprised if Veronica had maxed it out.

"What are you talking about?"

"His card was declined at the store."

"Oh?"

"Yes. I need to let him know as soon as possible."

Veronica examined her nails. "You can. It won't make a difference. The card has been closed."

"How do you know?" Then Erica understood. Veronica was responsible for this fiasco. She felt like wrapping her hands around Cruella's neck. "What the fuck are you trying to pull? I'm grabbing all these clothes, bringing them up to the cash register, only to waste the store's time. You're a real asshole, you know that?"

Veronica smirked. "I'm sure you didn't need those clothes anyway." She pushed her hair over her shoulder. "You'd better get used to it. The free ride is coming to a close."

Erica went up to her. "Quit fucking with me or I'll make you regret it." She walked off before she snatched her weave off her head.

Chapter 12

Everybody Wants Something

It had been a long day for Byron or at least it felt that way after Veronica spent half of it complaining about Erica. He finally had to hide out in his studio to get away. Through his small window, the sun had long set behind the trees and the sky had turned dark purple. However, he wasn't focused on night—he was concentrating on his speakers.

Every now and then, Byron liked to listen to the radio to see what was popular. As he sat behind his desk, he wanted to vomit. The music—if you could call it that—was despicable. Who would buy it? *Idiots.* Tired of hearing the reason his career was no longer where it used to be, Byron pressed the button on his screen to end the torture. There had to be some way for him to get back on top in the industry. He had tried this country-living shit and it was not working. He missed his world. The question remained: did his world miss him?

Some things suggested that it did. Even though he wasn't working with any artists, unknowns and newcomers to music still raided his inbox asking for help. While getting his ego stroked from the emails, a different one popped up to the top. He would have ignored it, if it weren't for the exclamation mark on it. He clicked on the email to find a bill from a health care clinic and read *$1,215!* And the email came from Angie.

Byron picked up his phone to call his sister. She didn't answer the first time. So he immediately called her back. He would call her twenty times if he needed to. She finally picked up the phone, sounding groggy.

"No need to pretend like you're sleep. I know better."

"What?" she asked, refusing to drop the act.

"What is this bill you sent me?"

"Oh. That was from the pediatrician. She's still sick and he had to run a few tests."

"Are you going there to hang out?"

"No. It's not that bad."

"Are you serious? Look. I understand that I promised to help you with the bills, but you need to stop running to the doctor for everything. Did Mama do that with us?"

"No, she couldn't afford to."

"And neither can you." Byron was serious. He didn't want his sister using him for money. He'd always given her whatever she asked for. However, this was ridiculous. He didn't want her using this situation to play him.

"All I'm trying to do is hold up my end of the bargain. Next time she's crying and running a fever in the middle of the night, I'll let her die."

"Quit being dramatic. All I'm asking is for you to lay off the medical bills. Is that too much?"

Angie sighed. "I guess not."

"You need to go get one of those books on home remedies. There's no need for all of this."

"I gotta go." Angie hung up before Byron could say anything else.

His sister was definitely angry with him. He didn't care. She needed some self-control. He'd talk to her later. Maybe he would feel better once he took a shower. Byron stood from his chair and went upstairs.

He entered his immaculate master bathroom. White marble floor. Two large plants near the wall and two smaller plants behind the Jacuzzi shaped tub. Byron's spirit dropped when he saw Veronica sitting with bubbles surrounding her right under the tub's arch.

She threw him a sexy smile. "I've been waiting for you."

He could tell by the look on Veronica's face that she had, and this time she would not be denied. He had been trying to avoid any further baby conversations. It had worked until now. The fireplace behind Veronica was gently lit casting a warm glow around her face and her loose bun. She was working extra hard.

"Aren't you going to join me?" she asked.

He shook his head. "I'm really tired. I was thinking about taking a shower and hoping in the bed."

She pushed her bottom lip out into a pout. "If I didn't know any better, I'd think you weren't attracted to me anymore."

Byron rolled his eyes. "Don't be ridiculous." He shrugged out of his suspenders.

"C'mon. If you get in, I can give you a back rub. Maybe that will help."

He could not resist her forever, even though this smelled like a pregnancy ploy. Byron slid off his clothes and navigated over to the tub. He put one foot in and pulled it back out.

Veronica laughed. "Sorry. I'm used to it."

"You could have warned me you were bathing in crab boil."

She laughed again. He eased his foot in, and this time he was prepared for the hot temperature. After he sat, Veronica leaned back and instructed him to do the same. He did and closed his eyes. He really did get tired a lot faster these days, which meant nothing when he had a much younger wife who was hardly ever tired. She didn't have to work or think, just look pretty. She rubbed his shoulders and his chest. This seemed like a good time to ask her about something that's been on his mind.

"What can you tell me about Shaun ending up at the party?" Byron asked while his eyes were still closed. He could feel Veronica shrug.

"I don't know. I told you he wasn't on the list."

"Why didn't you tell me he was here?"

"I, I thought maybe you had a change of heart and allowed him to come."

Byron opened his eyes and turned to look at her. "You know better than that."

She sighed. "So I didn't want any drama. I figured if I didn't ring the alarm nothing bad would happen."

"But it did."

"I had no way of knowing that. I mean, yeah, Erica isn't the most elegant person in the world. I still didn't expect that."

Her ragging on his daughter was getting old. Byron glared at her. "Let me set something straight. Erica will always be my daughter, whether you approve of her or not. She's my family. And no one is allowed in this house unless I OK it. If you're not sure, ask me. Is that clear?"

She frowned. "Fine."

He turned back around, leaned his head back and closed his eyes again. Silence hung in the air. Byron figured that Veronica's feelings were hurt. She'd get over it. He had to put her in her place. Besides, he didn't believe that she didn't know Shaun was coming. He just couldn't prove it. One thing was for sure—he didn't want that to ever happen again.

Veronica finally broke the silence. "Guess what?" she said, like she was singing a song.

"What?"

"I'm ovulating."

I knew it. What else would she have to say to him? The only thing she wanted to do was have another baby.

"Why are you so obsessed with having a baby all of a sudden?"

"Isn't it time?"

"How you figure?"

"We've been married over five years. Surely, this is a good time to have a baby. We have everything we want. Why not share it with a child?"

He remained silent. He didn't feel the same. There was no need to add to the family. He couldn't see himself putting time or interest in it.

She continued. "It would be like starting all over again. You don't think we'd have a beautiful child."

She eased her hand down his chest and toward his groin. She played with him under the water. His member stood at attention, despite any protest he could give to her baby request or otherwise. He couldn't complain. He was happy it still worked without prescribed medication. She nibbled on his neck. He turned red. She moved in front of him and wrapped her legs around him. Before long, she was bouncing on him. She kept him going until she climaxed. Then he followed suit. Almost as quickly as it started, it was over.

Chapter 13

Give Me What I Want

Erica couldn't get over how slick Veronica thought she was. She would pay for cutting off that card to make her look like a fool. Erica had half a mind to body slam her to the floor the next time she saw her. No one played with her like that. She would never forgive her.

She hadn't had a chance to tell her dad about it. So she woke up that morning looking for him. After looking in several of his common spots in the house, it finally hit her. Erica went down to the studio. She found her father sitting in his chair at the boards, where she had seen him so many times while she was growing up. Music was coming through the large speakers. She paused for a minute to consider if she should enter his sanctuary. His other world.

Erica decided it was important to let him know that Veronica had overstepped her boundaries. She walked up to her dad. He saw her and cut the music off.

"What's up?" he asked.

"I wanted to talk to you for a minute." He spun around in his chair to face her. "Did you know that Veronica canceled your credit card?" Erica asked.

He sighed. "Which card?"

"The one I use."

"I don't know of any cards being canceled."

"Well," Erica crossed her arms, "she did and I think you should set her straight."

"My question is how do you know she canceled it?"

"How else? I tried to use it."

"For what?"

"Clothes. What else?"

"You have clothes. A whole room full of clothes." Her father laced his hands and rested them over his stomach.

"What are you saying?"

"That you didn't need to buy anything else. It's interesting how I tell you to move out within two months and you want to go shopping."

Why did he have to lecture her now? He was totally missing the point. "Are you going to do something about her taking the card away?"

He shrugged. "Maybe. But you need to get focused. What are you gonna do?"

It was time for her to leave him to his music. "I'm gonna let you finish what you were doing 'cause this is not going right."

Her father turned back to his boards and cranked the volume up on some music she'd never heard before. She couldn't understand why her father would be so oblivious to her. There was no way he was cutting her all the way off. Yet it was clear that she would need to get the money for Leon from somewhere, especially as things got tighter around the house. She decided to take Alonzo up on his offer. See how serious he was about being there for her. Let her find out he was blowing smoke and

Erica would fix him too. She went the nice route and called to check on him, but there was no answer. She tried texting and he still hadn't responded.

At this point, it had been a couple of days since their rendezvous in the car and his uncle's boat. She didn't want Alonzo to think she was all over him. He really wasn't her type. He was a bit older. He was stockier than she was used to. She wasn't totally attracted to him. At the same time, she didn't mind keeping up with him in hopes that he could fix her money woes. In exchange, he could get her time. That would work for her. First he had to respond to her calls.

Fed up, she gave it a rest. She would check with her father to see if he knew what happened to Alonzo. Erica threw on some short shorts and an orange blouse and headed down to the kitchen to bake. When she felt stressed, cooking calmed her. As soon as she came downstairs, she gasped. "What are you doing here?"

Alonzo walked toward her from the hallway, as if he didn't have a care in the world. "I'm here to see your father." He cupped his hands together.

She squinted her eyes. This was all a game. He was there for her, but wanted to make it seem like he didn't care if he saw her. "So you're only here to see my daddy?"

"Yes. We have a meeting today."

She nodded. *Two could play this game.* "Have a good one." Erica trotted to the kitchen and opened the cabinet doors, ignoring his presence.

Alonzo turned to walk off. Something in her became angry. How dare he turn his back on her? She wasn't some bird he could treat any kind of way. "I hope you're not expecting to get any more," she shouted.

He paused at her words, but kept walking away. She knew he was way thirstier than he wanted to let on. His pride and ego wouldn't let him admit it. Erica stayed out of the way while he met with her daddy. While her lemon cake was baking in the oven, she decided to go back to her room and change into a red, white, and blue bikini. She topped it off with some Luis Vuitton heels to stroll outside on the patio and lay near the pool. It would be hard for him to miss seeing her when he left the mansion.

Erica chuckled as she stretched out and took in the afternoon rays. Alonzo thought he was so smart. She knew how to make him drool. She put on her Gucci shades and earbuds and closed her eyes. She had at least another forty minutes before she had to check on her cake. Her phone would alert her when it was ready. She got into her music, keeping her eyes closed. She didn't even open them when she finally heard the front door open. Erica felt a shadow over her. She was certain it was Alonzo.

"Stop acting like you don't know I'm here," he said.

She sighed. "What do you want?"

"You know what I want."

"Whatever. You came to see my dad, remember?"

"You're a very bad girl."

She shrugged. Her eyes were still closed.

"I have something for that."

Erica chuckled out loud.

"Laugh now. You won't be laughing later."

"I don't want it unless there's something in it for me." *Bargaining time.*

"Something like what?"

Erica finally opened her eyes and lifted her sunglasses. "You said tell you if I needed anything, right?"

He shrugged.

"Well, I do."

Alonzo put his hands in his pockets. "What do you need?"

"What do we all need?" she batted her eyelashes.

He looked into the distance. "Money."

She took her sunglasses off and used the ear part to trace around her breasts. When he returned his attention to her, his eyes dutifully followed her movements. Like a dog on a leash.

He cleared his throat. "How much?"

"Three thousand." Of course, she only needed $2,000 for Leon, but who said she shouldn't make a little extra out of these negotiations? Call it damages for the game he was playing on her.

"What do you have? Gambling debts?"

"A girl's got expenses. Yay or nay?" Erica licked her lips to seal the deal.

Chapter 14

I Got You

Alonzo bent Erica over the bed and pummeled her. Erica moaned uncontrollably. She knew he couldn't resist her. It made her feel powerful. Like she was in control. She also didn't mind his company. It didn't hurt that he was helping her out with Leon's money. She still wasn't in love with him, and she never would be, but for now what they were doing worked for her.

When he was done, he slapped her on the butt and climbed off of her. She lay breathing hard. He lay next to her and scanned her.

"Hit the spot, huh?"

She slapped him on the chest, and he chuckled. She closed her eyes, not to go to sleep but to enjoy the silence and peace.

Alonzo broke the silence. "What do you want?"

"Rest." Maybe she could get it if he stopped talking.

"No. I mean, what are you really looking for?"

She moaned. On second thought, maybe it was time she gathered her things to go. "I don't know." She rolled over and got a quick glance at where her things were lying. It wouldn't take her too long to get her clothes back on.

"That's not an answer."

"It's the only one I got."

"You've got to be thinking about your future some time."

In response, Erica sat up and started pulling at her dress. "I don't worry about the future. It'll give you gray hairs."

He smirked. "That's not true."

"Sure it is." She stood. She'd had about enough of this. She didn't need a shrink or someone to analyze her and her future. Erica was there to have fun and get some money. That was it. Clearly, the fun was over and so was her visit. She pulled the edge of her dress down passed her knees.

"Where are you going?" he asked.

"I need to get going before my father gets worried."

"He still worries about you?"

She nodded. "Of course."

He propped himself up on the bed with his elbow. "If you get married, maybe he won't be."

She laughed. "I'm a long way from matrimony."

"How do you know? It might be right around the corner."

Erica rolled her eyes. Now it *was* really time to get out of there. She didn't need him playing games with her head like she was some poor little girl who'd been waiting for a man to come along and marry her. Save the day. Marriage was the last thing she wanted. It looked like too much trouble. Look at her dad. He was married and most of the time he looked unhappy.

"I'm good." She slid on her shoes.

"OK." His tone changed slightly. She heard it but decided not to make a big deal out of it. He was a big boy. He could handle her honesty.

"But you know you can't run forever. You have to be tamed eventually," he added.

"I don't have to do anything but be me. It's a take-it-or-leave-it situation."

Alonzo stood and blocked the door. Erica put her hand on her hip and waited for him to move. When he didn't, she tapped him on the chest. "Are you going to move or what?" she asked.

He slowly moved out of her way. She left him looking stupid. When she jumped in her dad's black Audi, she glanced at the clock. It was only 10:18 p.m. She pulled out her phone and called Leon.

"Are you awake?" she asked him.

"Yeah. Why?"

"Is the card there?"

"Came today."

"Good. I have your money."

"You can swing by."

Leon directed her to his house, which was a modest single family home. A white sedan was in the driveway, parked in front of a garage that looked like it hadn't been opened in years. The house had old screens on the windows and four steps leading to the front door. Two small chairs were on the porch. As she took the last step, she noticed a flower bed that badly needed tending. She couldn't remember ever living in this type of house. She thought he said he worked with her father, but, then again, he may not be as actively working as he was before. She shrugged it off and walked up to his front door. He answered her knocks and let her in.

"Where's the card?" she asked. He handed her the envelope, and she briefly inspected it to see if he opened it. Everything looked intact. "Here's the $2,000." She placed the money in his hand, minus her share.

Leon licked his thumb and started counting it. She took that time to open the mail and retrieve her credit card. She smiled. Now she had something to work with.

"It's all here," Leon said.

She turned to face him. "Of course, it is. You thought I would cheat you?"

"No." He smirked.

She twisted her lips to the side. "Right." Erica scanned his house. "Nice place."

He nodded. "Thanks."

"How long have you been here?"

"A few months."

"Why here?" Erica found it strange that he was in the music industry and he moved near Westbrook. "There's no music being made out here. Not like New York, LA, or Atlanta."

"I know some guys in this area."

"They must have a long way to go. No one with any real shot would come here."

Leon stared at the floor without saying much. Maybe she had said the wrong thing. She didn't mean to talk about his friends. "Hey. If you believe in them, they must be some good."

After an uncomfortable silence, Erica inched toward the door. "I need to get home. Pass my bedtime."

He walked her to the door. "Say, um, thanks for the money. It'll be a big help. As a matter of fact, I'm in transition right now. So every little bit helps."

"You're welcome."

"I'm a little behind on the rent. This will cover that. I also gotta get my car fixed. You think you'll be able to help me with it?"

Erica narrowed her eyes. Why would he ask her for more money when she just gave him some? If he was that hard up, he needed to get a job or win the lottery.

"I'm sorry. All I have is this card, and I'm gonna need to transition myself."

He stared at her as if he were expecting her to give him a second answer. That wasn't going to happen. She resented him asking her, a woman, for money. She already gave him more than he deserved. She needed to get out of there as soon as possible. Leon seemed to have more issues than she realized.

Chapter 15

Why Is This Happening?

Veronica had made it a restless night. So the following day, Byron locked himself in his office to keep anyone from coming in, especially her. He couldn't stand the idea of another conversation about having a baby. It was taking all he had not to scream that he didn't want one. He'd already had a baby and didn't feel the need to live that part of his life over again. Besides, his first baby turned out very different from his expectations. No reason to go through that again.

He wasn't a fool either. Veronica wanted a baby to make sure she had money, even if the marriage ended. He wasn't new to women doing that. Byron married her because he knew her well. He was pretty sure he was ahead of her in more ways than she realized. Unfortunately, his admission that he didn't want a baby would make relations tough around the house. It would come out sooner or later, though.

Byron stretched out on his couch and closed his eyes, breathing deeply, almost lulling himself into a nice afternoon nap. Before he could completely relax, he heard a buzzing sound. He opened his eyes and saw that someone was calling his phone. He reached for it on the nearby table.

Byron saw his sister's name pop up on his cell phone. He chose to ignore it. The call ended but immediately started ringing all over again. He sighed and picked it up.

"I need more."

"Angie . . ."

"She's in the hospital. This time, it's Inflammatory Bowel Disease."

He swore Angie was making this shit up. "I don't have time for this."

"Neither do I. You gave the baby to me and it's my responsibility. I'm telling you I need some financial help here."

"That's it. I want to meet with these doctors."

"What?"

"Yes."

She stuttered. "Fine. Come here, if you don't believe me. I'm telling you. This kid has a lot of problems. No way I could make this up."

Byron told Angie he was on his way. Before he hung up, he insisted she give him the number to the doctor. While he was on the way to the hospital, he told the doctor he would need to speak with him in person upon his arrival. Byron didn't allow room for the doctor to refuse. So the doctor obliged.

Shortly after Byron arrived, he and Angie were ushered into a waiting room. A couple of babies started yelling as soon as they sat down. Byron bounced his leg while he sat waiting for the doctor to see them privately. He had better things to do with his time than meet a pediatrician and get attacked by the sound of screaming babies. When the doctor's assistant finally took them to his office, the tall, slender man seemed apologetic.

"Thank you for waiting. It's been a busy day, but I wanted to make your request," Dr. Doug Wilson said.

Byron frowned. "It's an urgent matter that needs attention."

"Absolutely. Have a seat." They all sat. "I understand you have concerns about Megan's health."

"More like poor health," Byron said.

Angie jumped in. "Sorry, Doctor. This is my brother, Byron. He's been helping me with the bills for the baby. As I'm sure you can appreciate, it's a struggle taking care of all of this myself."

The doctor gave her a gentle smile. "Yes. I know it's hard. I see many families in this situation."

Angie nodded. "Luckily, my brother has been able to keep me from going in the hole."

Dr. Wilson raised his eyebrows. "That's nice. I think everything will clear up soon."

"But he has some questions for you about Megan and all the trouble she's having." Angie twisted her fingers.

"What's going on? My sister is hitting me up regularly about this test and that procedure. I can't keep up."

Dr. Wilson nodded. "I see. She's gotten a few infections here or there. At this point, it doesn't seem to be a reason for alarm. We're trying to determine if they are related issues or if one is triggering the other. However, I really do think this will all be over soon."

"What's wrong with her now?" Byron asked.

"She has Inflammatory Bowel Disease."

"Which means?"

"She has diarrhea, fever and severe abdominal pain."

"It's not fatal, right?"

"Oh, no. Just very uncomfortable."

"How did she get this?"

"It could be diet. There may be a chance its heredity. Do you have a relative that has suffered from this?" Dr. Wilson looked between Angie and Byron.

Byron shook his head.

Angie hit his upper arm. "Grandma Sally."

Now that he thought about it, she may have had some stomach issues. He wasn't really paying attention. Growing up, Byron wanted to roam and find himself. That didn't include staying at home or watching his grandmother go back and forth to the bathroom. He nodded. "Yeah, I guess. So how are you going to treat it?"

"We're going to put her on some anti-diarrheal medication. It's a little formula that can be mixed and given to her in a bottle."

"And what if that doesn't work?" Byron asked. So far, it seemed like nothing was working. He figured he might as well ask ahead of time.

"The methods we're trying should work. If by chance it doesn't, our worst-case scenario is that we have to perform surgery."

"Hopefully, that doesn't happen," Angie said.

"We are doing all we can for Megan. She's had some issues, but we're here to support her."

Byron believed he was pretty good at looking beyond what's being said. He had a feeling that his sister was going to be coming back to him for more money. He shouldn't have listened to Erica. When she stalled on giving the baby up for adoption, he should have started the paperwork anyway. Not waited for her to change her mind. Look what she'd gotten them into. Had she given it up in the beginning, the hospital trips wouldn't even be an issue. Now he was stuck shelling out money for a sick baby all the time. The bills were getting steep. He had to find a way to put a stop to this before his sister and this baby bled him dry.

Chapter 16

What Relationship?

Erica started upstairs but stopped when she saw her dad in the den, nibbling on her lemon cake. She hadn't seen him all day. She couldn't resist going in to mess with him.

"I thought we weren't supposed to eat in the den," she said.

He chewed slowly. "Mind your business."

She laughed and sat. "I know I cook better than Veronica." Come to think of it, Erica couldn't remember the last time she saw her go anywhere near the stove or oven.

Daddy licked a couple of cake crumbs off his lips. "What are you doing here? Surprised you're not somewhere painting the town red."

"I don't party every night."

"Humph."

"What does that mean?"

He balled the wrapper up and placed it on the table. It slowly started to open back up. "It means you need to get more serious about life."

"I am. I've already started looking at places."

"Where?"

"Why? You don't believe me?"

"No, I don't. And what's going on with you and Alonzo?"

Erica swallowed hard. "What are you talking about?"

"I've seen you two talking a couple of times. What are you talking about?"

"It was only polite hellos. He's your friend."

Daddy fixed his eyes on her. Of course, he didn't buy it.

"I'm focused on getting things in order, since you're kicking me out."

"I'm forcing you to leave the nest. Test your wings. You'll like it better."

Erica wasn't convinced. Even though she managed to get a credit card and some extra money, she still felt insecure about moving out on her own. Twenty-five thousand would only stretch so far. Then what? Keep using someone like Alonzo for money? She didn't know how much longer this fling they had would last. There would always be another man, but how long would she want to do that? She hung her head at the thought. "I don't know."

"Whatever you do, make sure you're making good choices. You're getting to an age where the wrong decision could have dire consequences. Everything can't be swept under the rug like this baby and that's not even working out that well."

"What?"

Daddy sighed. "Angie has been calling me a lot about money to take care of all these medical bills for the girl."

"Is she OK?"

Erica's father raised an eyebrow at her. She glanced down. Her question rushed out quickly, betraying her earnest concern for the baby she carried for nine months.

"Yes," he answered.

"Then what's wrong with her?"

"Nothing, really. Some bowel problems."

"Oh, no."

"She'll be fine. It's Angie I'm more concerned about. If she hits me up for another dollar . . ." he allowed his words to trail off.

"I thought you were going to help take care of her." Erica's tone was becoming accusatory. Based on the expression on her father's face, he noticed.

"That's what I'm doing . . . but when your aunt keeps coming to me asking for money to pay for this test and that test, I have to inquire."

"So something is wrong." Erica was overcome with grief and guilt. Somehow this was her fault. Her child was sick. Was it because she knew her mother wasn't there to hold her and sing her lullabies until she fell asleep? The little girl would probably be better, if Erica were to go see her. It was too bad she couldn't bring herself to do it. She couldn't face this awful reminder that she had been violated in the worse way, even though—in her opinion—giving up her child made her less than a woman.

"I told you, girl. She'll be fine. The things wrong with her are minor. Your aunt is trying to collect. That's all and I'mma keep an eye on it."

Erica said, "Do me a favor . . . keep me updated on her."

***

Her father's words were still ringing in her ear the whole time she was with Alonzo that night. He had called her and insisted on taking her out on an official date. Erica finally obliged. She made him choose something simple. They decided on a movie with dinner afterward. She appreciated the noise from the screen. It prevented Alonzo from talking to her and asking what was wrong. He already asked that question a couple of times in the car. She could sit in her thoughts and feign interest in the movie.

It had been a few months since she'd really thought about the baby she gave away and that made her feel even more guilty, after hearing about the issues it was going through. She was grateful for the

147

chance to move on from the pregnancy, yet her father's words reminded her that her past would always be trailing behind her like toilet paper stuck to her shoe. Sometimes it felt more like a thorn in her soul. She couldn't pluck it out, no matter how hard she tried. That angered her even more.

The movie ended and she couldn't remember one scene from it. Alonzo, on the other hand, wanted to talk about the movie as soon as they got in the car. Meanwhile, Erica was so distracted she didn't even think to put her seatbelt on.

"That wasn't bad. The acting could have been better. The plot was pretty solid. What do you think?"

Erica sighed. "It was alright."

"What did you like about it?"

She felt herself getting irritated—similar to the way she did the night they first got together in his car. "Not much. It's an average movie."

Alonzo pulled off. It started to sprinkle on the windshield as they rode farther down the street. After a few minutes, he stared at her. "You've been distant all night. Is everything OK?"

"Everything," Erica caught herself about to raise her voice, "everything is fine. I guess I'm tired tonight."

"How could you be tired? You don't work."

Then maybe I'm tired of you. "It hasn't been a good day."

"So you're going to ruin the night?"

If she didn't know any better she would think he was picking a fight with her. "No, I'm not trying to. I'm just not in the mood."

Alonzo nodded. "Are you waiting for me to kiss your ass again?"

"Are you kidding? How about asking me why I'm feeling so shitty? Maybe that would get a better result."

"How about communicating it on your own? You're not a baby. It's time to be more proactive and mature in this relationship."

"Who the hell said we were in a relationship? Huh?"

With that question, Alonzo was finally silent. She had him where she wanted him.

"You think because we've fucked a few times that makes us Will and Jada?" She laughed. "Hilarious. I don't even know you. Asking about my future. What about your past? Why did you really move here? How about that?"

Erica was on a roll. He wanted her to open up and talk. That's exactly what she'd do. It wouldn't be what he wanted to hear, which would be his fault. Pushing her to speak. The least he could have done was show concern for her. Yet he had the nerve to insinuate that they were in a relationship.

"All of this because I asked you why the fuck you're so tired after doing nothing all day?" Alonzo's eyebrows drew together as if they were knitting.

"That's none of your business. So what I'm not working. Are you? Where is this deal with you and my dad? I haven't heard anything about it yet."

"That's none of your business. You should know I'm not spending all this time and money on a chick that's messing with somebody else."

Erica turned to look out the window. It was pouring, and she could only see the blurred lights from the store and street lights they passed along the way. She would not be baited. He was fishing for confirmation on whether she was dating someone else. He would have to keep wondering. If she gave him reassurance now, she would always have to guarantee they were exclusive. To be honest, she didn't believe she would ever commit to him. She would not lie.

"Oh, you don't have nothing to say, huh?"

"Sure. Got any friends?"

Alonzo sped up his car. She figured he was in a rush to get her home. That was his problem. He started this argument. Suddenly he squealed at the side of the road. The tires took several feet too finally stop.

"Get out." His voice was monotone and he looked straight through the window shield.

Erica crossed her arms. He was crazy if he thought she would get out in this rain. "I'm not going anywhere. You take my ass home."

Alonzo reached over and opened the passenger door. "Get out." He pushed her shoulder.

She maneuvered away from him. "Stop it. I'm not going anywhere."

Then he faced Erica and gave her the hardest shove she'd ever experienced. She rolled over and went tumbling out of the car.

Chapter 17

What's the Problem?

Byron was still in shock. When Erica came home wet and angry, he couldn't do much to calm her down, but he could gather that something went terribly wrong. She wouldn't give any straight answers. Only a bunch of yelling. He finally had to send her to her room to calm down.

Once he found out that she had been out with Alonzo, he really had to get down to the bottom of this. He was under the impression that they were hitting it off. That's one of the reasons he pretended to be suspicious to their budding relationship when talking to her. He figured that would keep her interested in Alonzo longer. Since she was so attracted to danger, Byron thought that feeding the idea that he was forbidden would make him more appealing to Erica. His plan was working. After tonight, Alonzo would never even think of harming Byron's daughter again.

Byron took a deep breath to calm himself down. With his daughter, the truth could be almost anything. So he would investigate at dinner. He pulled a jacket over his white shirt and black pants.

"Shit." Veronica said as she walked into the bedroom.

"What's the problem?"

"I'm still not pregnant." She poked out her lip. He hated it when she did that.

He picked imaginary lint off his jacket. "Don't worry. It takes time. It'll happen."

Byron could feel her looking at him, analyzing his response. "Don't you want a younger child?

"It doesn't matter."

She sighed. He yawned.

"Sleepy?" she asked.

"Yep. It was hard to go to sleep after all of that yelling Erica did last night."

"I wonder what really happened."

"That's what I'm gonna find out."

"She probably gave him too much lip."

"It doesn't matter. No man has the right to lay a finger on her." Byron frowned. "I can't believe I have to tell you this." He really couldn't believe that he had to say that.

"Of course. A man cannot hit a woman without paying for it."

"I liked Alonzo. I even thought he'd be a good man for Erica. We gotta clear the air about this situation." His tone was calm and assured.

"Uh, do you think that's really going to work? I mean, she doesn't like exclusivity."

"I think she hasn't met the right man."

"And you really think Alonzo might be right for her?"

"It was a possibility until this incident."

"How do you know if he even wants her?"

"Oh, he wants her."

"How do you know?"

"I'm a man and I know."

Byron had already figured that Alonzo was a man that wanted to go places in life. When you have a man like that, he'll do just about anything to get ahead, even marrying a wealthy man's daughter. While he may have been getting ahead of himself, slightly, Byron was certain he had pegged Alonzo right. He'd seen the way he stared at Byron's big house and expensive possessions. He likely fantasized about this being his house when he walked up the driveway. That was the type of thing he could use and hang over Alonzo's head in regards to Erica and their potential partnership.

A buzz came from the intercom. Byron pressed the button.

"He's here," Lana said.

Byron glanced in the mirror one last time before going downstairs to meet with Alonzo. Lana had led him to Byron's office as instructed. When he walked into the room, Alonzo stood from the couch. Byron waved him back down.

"Hello, sir. Thank you for the invitation."

Byron sat in the chair behind his desk without offering any warm acknowledgement. Strictly business.

Alonzo wiped some of the sweat off his brow. "I know you must have some concerns."

Byron leaned forward and laced his fingers together on the desk.

Alonzo swallowed hard. "Last night was a misunderstanding."

"How so?" Byron asked.

He stammered. "We got into an argument and the next thing I know, she fell out of the car."

"Son," Byron started, "I'm giving you a chance to tell me the truth. Take it."

"I don't know if the door was unlocked or what, but I looked up and she was falling."

Byron felt his pulse quicken. He stilled his growing anger. That was the only way to be calm enough to get his point across. "Why didn't you go back and get her?"

"I had to drive up the street and turn around. When I did, she was running the other way. I guessed she was calling someone to pick her up." Alonzo stared at the floor. "We said some pretty ugly things to each other. I figured she didn't want to ride with me any farther. I couldn't blame her. I really am sorry, sir."

Byron didn't buy anything Alonzo was saying. There was also something about his mannerisms that seemed quite insincere. He leaned back in his chair and hit a button to lock his office door. "When I was starting out in the business, I was working under this asshole executive. He had strange ways of testing people. He'd call at odd hours and demand that I get in the studio and when I got there, all the sessions were empty. One day, I decided to confront him about it and explain that I didn't appreciate it. You know what he told me?"

Alonzo shook his head.

"He said he was my boss, and if I wanted to work in this business, I'd better do whatever he said, whenever he said to do it. I shouldn't have even questioned him, right? I put it behind me and continued to learn my craft. I bought some production equipment. Must have been about $3,500, way more than I could afford. A couple of weeks later, I noticed it was missing. I freaked out. I accused everybody until the executive mailed me a big box, and when I opened it, I found the equipment with a note that said. 'Thanks for letting me borrow it. My son liked playing on it.'" Byron reached into his drawer and pulled out his Smith & Wesson.

Alonzo's eyes grew to the size of saucers and he started to move around in his chair. He looked like he wanted to run, but the man in him forced him to take what was coming like he was supposed to.

Byron appeared oblivious to Alonzo's rising discomfort and continued the story. "So I went to his office, locked him in, and had a nice chat with him. Me, him, and Wesson. I didn't have any more problems." He rubbed the smooth steel on his gun. "I told that story to ask you this: if I would do that over my equipment, what do you think I would do about my daughter?"

"Sir, I'm sorry about last night. It won't happen again. I assure you," Alonzo said.

Byron pointed the gun his way. "I'm going to hold you to that. Because if she comes back to me about a situation like this—"

Alonzo shook his head. "No way, sir."

He got his point across. "Good. Glad to hear it," Byron said.

Lana knocked on the door. "Dinner is served."

"Be right there," Byron shouted to make sure she could hear him through the door. He slowly put his gun away and pressed a button to unlock the door. Alonzo let out a slow but definite sigh of relief.

Byron, Veronica, Alonzo, and Erica sat in the dining room. The mood was solemn, like a funeral. No laughter. No smiles. They sat quietly. The room was dimly lit.

"So how is everything?" Veronica looked at Alonzo. Her words were stiff and hollow.

"It's been better," Alonzo muttered.

Dinner was placed in front of them. Veal and asparagus. While others feigned interest in their plates, Byron stared holes into Alonzo's head. Occasionally, he caught it and squirmed in his chair.

"How long have you been seeing each other now?" Veronica asked.

Alonzo cleared his throat. "Almost a month,"

"Are you in love?" she asked.

Erica rolled her eyes. "Really?"

Byron wanted to hear this.

"I'll answer," Alonzo said, "While Erica and I hadn't been seeing each other long, I am fond of her . . . I deeply regret yesterday."

"What about you?" she looked at Erica.

"Are you?" Erica said.

"I think that's enough, Veronica. No need to give these kids the third degree on their feelings," Byron said. He'd heard enough. The way Erica stood, it looked like she had too.

Chapter 18

I've Had Enough

"I'm not gonna do this," Erica said. She couldn't stay there any longer and listen to Alonzo pretend like he did nothing wrong. Like this was some horrible accident. He pushed her out of the car. She would not allow that to be dismissed.

Erica stormed away from the table, ignoring the call for her to come back and settle down. She was so upset she had to go off somewhere and clear her head. She went upstairs and changed clothes. She figured going to the gym to work out would calm her down. On her way there, Alonzo called and texted her several times. She refused to answer.

The gym was a good idea. Getting on the stairs, the treadmill and the pullups helped put her mind at ease. She was composed again. She stopped to take a sip on her bottle of water.

Out of the corner of her eye, she saw a man looking at her. She glanced over and sized him up. He was fairly tall and lanky. Sweat glistened off his sculpted arms. She took another chug of water to give herself a chance to observe him. He made his way over to her.

"I admire your workout," he said.

She turned away from him without saying anything. He kept talking.

"Everybody doesn't come in here to get it the way you do and the results show."

Erica remained silent.

"I'm sorry. Allow me to introduce myself. I'm Carlos, a personal trainer here."

She looked at his black muscle shirt and basketball shorts. He followed her gaze and chuckled. "I know. I'm not in my usual uniform. Today is my off day."

"And you came to work anyway?" she asked.

"I still need to work out."

So clearly, he didn't have a lot of money or he would have a gym at home. *Don't judge.*

He offered his hand. She looked at it for a second. It was strong and muscular, like the rest of him. He could be a trainer. She reluctantly gave him her hand to shake. He shook hers sturdily. Not too hard. He also gave her a smile. She didn't return it.

"What's your name?" he asked.

"E." Sounded corny, but she still didn't know him and didn't feel like giving him her full name.

"E?" He smiled even harder. No doubt he must have known what she was doing. He nodded. "Nice to meet you, E."

She nodded.

"I noticed you're basically sticking to this equipment. Why don't I take you on a tour?"

"No thanks. I'm about done." She grabbed her water.

"That's fine. At least you'll know when you come back. It'll only take a few minutes and it's worth it."

Something in his words told her she should oblige. So she did. Erica walked beside him as he led her to other equipment in the large gym. He pointed out machines, what they do and how they help. She only half listened while he continued to talk and attempt to charm her with his wit. She decided to ask him the question that had been lingering in her mind.

"You said you work here. I don't remember seeing you here before," Erica said.

"I haven't seen you either or else I would have been said hello and offered my help. I usually work the night shift."

"I come in during the day. Morning."

"Well, you're doing a good job. I just saw that you stuck to certain machines. Sticking to the same equipment isn't exciting enough. I often see people lose steam and stop coming to the gym. They get bored. You know?"

"Yeah. I used to exercise at home. Now I do it here to get out of the house."

"Because it's different, right?"

She nodded. Actually, it was the only way she could get away from Veronica. He didn't need to hear all of that.

"To keep it original and interesting, we have to add variety. That's the key to fitness and most things in life," he said.

"That's true."

They reached the end of the equipment. He pulled out a bunch of keys. "Want to see the classes?"

"Sure."

He walked her around the corner to a bunch of rooms. There were at least seven doors down the hall. All of them were purple. He opened the first door and showed her a room with hard wood floors and ceiling to floor mirrors. There was multicolored light in the shape of a ball hanging from the ceiling.

"Are all of your classes in rooms like this?" she asked.

"More or less. They vary depending on the class that's in there. Next door is the cycle room."

They left the first room and visited the room full of cycles. The other rooms allowed for different types of fitness activities, some of which required a screen for the client to interact with an instructor from afar.

Carlos took her into the last room and closed the door behind them. There was nothing in there but a table in the far corner.

"What do you do in here?" she asked, frowning.

"They haven't decided yet. The owner is thinking of adding some new programs. He doesn't know which one so they are keeping it open for right now."

"How about making it a room where someone can exercise alone? Put some equipment in here. Let them have their own music and they can just go."

He raised his eyebrows. "That's not a bad idea. I'll bring that up to management." He walked closer to her. "If they do that, does it mean that I won't see you out front anymore?"

"It depends."

He stepped closer. "On what?"

She scanned his body. It *was* nice. "My mood. Sometimes I don't feel like being bothered. This would allow me to be by myself, if I feel like it."

"What about now?" He stared at her. His brown eyes bore into hers. Erica matched the intensity of his stare, increasing it. He smirked. "I like you."

"That's all?" She put her hands on his firm pecks and felt herself getting excited.

Carlos put his hands around her waist and shook his head. "No."

He pulled her closer and kissed her, softly at first, and then he pressed his lips against hers firmer. She wrapped her hands around his neck, pulling him closer. He cupped her butt, squeezing. She moaned and stuck her tongue in his mouth. He returned the favor. Carlos walked her back toward the table in the corner. Once they reached it, he bent her backward. She lay her back on the table, staring at the ceiling.

She anxiously anticipated what would happen next. She looked forward to this escape. He lowered his gym shorts to reveal his penis standing at half mass, waiting for use. Erica pulled her exercise pants down, and he helped her get them all the way off. He opened her legs and slid inside of her. He pumped steadily, fitting her like a glove. Carlos eased his hands over her stomach and kissed it, and then he slid his hands under her sports bra and massaged her breasts. If they weren't complete strangers, it would have been romantic. But she didn't mind. With Carlos, there was no pressure. It was like that at the beginning of her relationship with Alonzo. Now it was feeling more like a chore. She appreciated the chance to have fun with Carlos. He was a perfect fit for her and exactly what she needed—right now. She smiled. He felt great. She lost track of time in that room.

Chapter 19

Secrets Kept

Erica finished her romp with Carlos, the trainer, and went back home. He'd done a lot to clear her mind. She had some perspective on what she needed to do. In a nutshell, she had to end it with Alonzo. Her father may have been able to entertain his fantasies, but she needed to cut her loses. She didn't even love him. Wasn't that supposed to count for something? She really wanted to get her life back on track. It seemed like she'd been out of balance ever since she got pregnant.

Erica entered the iron gates of her father's estate and hiked up the hill toward the house. She tugged her light, jacket around her as the breeze stiffened. On her way there, she heard rustling in the bushes. She wasn't sure it was anything. So she kept walking. Then she heard another noise. She couldn't quite make it out. This was usually the point in scary movies where the person who goes over to investigate gets killed, especially if it's a black actor, yet she felt compelled to go over and see what it was about. She didn't fear for her life because she knew how to defend herself. When she heard the noise again, she had to follow it.

Erica tiptoed over with her senses heightened for whatever she would find. It was dark with a little light coming from the distance. Luckily for her, Daddy had made light apart of the landscape for the house. Her eyes scanned between the trees looking for evidence of life. She didn't see anything. She was about to give up when she heard a voice. This time, she saw some movement as well. Erica moved slowly toward the movement. Finally, she could make it out. It was Veronica performing oral sex on the gardener, Jose. Erica's eyes grew wide and she covered her mouth. She couldn't believe it.

Her first instinct was to rush over, push Veronica to the ground and whip her ass. She stopped herself. She reached into her jacket pocket and snuck out her iPhone. She found a spot where there was some light coming from the yard and pressed on the screen. For safe measure, she took a few more pics in effort to get a really good shot-one that would show that it was indeed Veronica. She looked at the photos quickly, satisfied with a couple of them, and turned to leave. Erica was careful, trying not to step on a fallen branch or crackling leaf. She wanted to leave as quietly as she came. Once she was safely back onto the manicured lawn, she darted around the house. Her father would not believe what she saw. Luckily, she had proof.

Later that night, she lay in her bed, thinking. This had been some night. She had a hook up and caught Veronica cheating on her dad. She tried to tell him she was no good a long time ago. Erica wished he would've listened. Part of her wanted to run through the house with the pictures and show Daddy, but she didn't want to hurt his feelings. As harsh as he could be, he was human like everybody else. No one wanted to hear that their spouse was cheating. Then a thought hit her. Should she really leave her father alone with Cruella? Her cell phone rang. She looked at it and saw that it was Alonzo. *Perfect time to break it off.*

"I've been trying to reach you. Where have you been?" he started right away.

"I was out clearing my head."

"I see." Alonzo paused. "Are you still angry?"

Erica wanted to say yes, but, honestly, she wasn't. Her concerns had turned more to her father. "I don't know," she said.

"Will you at least accept my apology?"

"Why should I?"

"Because it's the Christian thing to do."

Erica stared at the phone. *No, he didn't.* "What the hell do you know about that?"

He chuckled. "Just trying to break the ice."

The attempt at levity did seem to lift the mood a little. She had a hard time resisting a smirk. Suddenly she wasn't so angry with Alonzo. She saw her part in their disagreement. She was most resistant to communication. He didn't know anything about what she was going through or what she had been through. Maybe she overreacted too.

"I think you misunderstood me," he said.

Erica remained silent. She sensed that more was coming.

"All I wanted was to know this is going somewhere. I like that you're cool. I don't like that you make it seem like you don't give a shit about what we're doing here and if that's the case, let me know. I don't want to waste my time."

"I need to move forward at my own pace," Erica said. "I don't move fast for nobody."

"How long do we wait?"

Erica kicked around time frames. She hated this type of pressure. She didn't want to give him a date for fear that it wouldn't be long enough.

Alonzo rephrased the question. "How much time do you need?"

"I don't know."

"I need some kind of barometer. I can't dangle in the wind forever. I'm not going to do that."

"Fine. Give me another couple of months." That should hold him for a while.

"Are you sure?"

About as sure as I'm going to be. "Yeah."

***

The next day, she was in the kitchen when the phone rang. Erica waited for someone to answer. No one did. Tired of the ringing, she decided to answer it herself.

"Erica?"

Her blood ran cold. She could not mistake that voice for anyone else's. It was her Aunt Angie. Her stomach dropped. "Ye-yeah," she stuttered.

"How is everything?"

"Fine." Erica looked around the corner, searching for someone to give the phone to so that she could end the call. So far, she wasn't finding anyone.

"The child is doing well. I thought you might want to know," Aunt Angie said.

Erica opened her mouth to speak but didn't get far. Her mind was flooded with questions to ask.

What's her favorite color? What's her favorite food? Does she have to sleep with the light on? But for the life of her, she couldn't bring herself to ask them. It was like she wasn't supposed to do so. She had no right.

Her aunt continued to talk despite her silence. "If you ever want to visit Megan, let me know."

"OK," was all Erica could muster.

"What are you up to now?"

"Uh, I was on my way out. Do you want to hold for Daddy?"

"Sure."

Erica put the phone down as if it had an infection. She would not hold on to it any longer. Finally, Lana walked back into the house. "Have you seen Daddy?"

"He left about five minutes ago. He'll be back soon," Lana said.

"My aunt is on the phone. Let her know that." Erica turned and left the room. She refused to pick that phone up again. Instead, she darted upstairs to get ready to meet with Alonzo.

Chapter 20

What Are You Gonna Do?

It was late evening before Erica found her father. He was down in his studio. He had his fingers on the controls, adjusting the output on some music. He looked like a different man behind the knobs. He was consumed and in his element. Until now, Erica didn't realize how much her father must miss the music world.

"Aren't you ready to go back?" Erica asked her father.

He turned, noticing her for the first time. He raised an eyebrow in apparent surprise. "To what?"

"This."

He shook his head.

"It may not be a bad idea," Erica said. Given the latest developments, maybe he needed to be more preoccupied. She wasn't certain he knew what type of wife he had. It might be good for him to stay busy.

He sighed. "I don't know. What about Alonzo? What are you gonna do?"

She shrugged. "Nothing."

"That's what I'm afraid of." He pressed a few buttons. "I take it you're over last night."

"What?" she asked, confused. Her mind raced through the events that took place.

"The dinner. Are you OK now?" he asked.

"Oh. Yeah, I had to get out of there. It was too much for me."

"What really happened?"

Erica crossed her arms, as if that would somehow help her keep the truth in. "We started talking about the future and he got angry because I didn't see one with him."

"What do you see?"

"I'm not sure yet."

"I know how I feel about the situation. When do *you* plan to decide?"

"Soon." Erica really didn't know when she would figure out what she planned to do with the rest of her life. She didn't think that was pertinent right now.

Daddy faced her. "Do you want to find a decent man to marry and settle down with?"

"Eventually."

"You need to decide that now."

"I'm too young."

"You weren't too young to get pregnant."

Ouch. She tightened her arms around herself. He didn't have to go there.

"What I'm saying is ... you're twenty-one. That's old enough to start behaving like an adult and adults get married."

Erica looked at the ground. She knew she was a disappointment to him, but all she could be was herself. No one else. If that wasn't enough, she didn't know what to tell him. "All I can do is make the right decision for me. Hopefully, that ends up being OK with you."

"You have less than two months now to get your life together. I will not enable you any longer. It's all fun and games until you wake up one day, twenty years from now, alone. Your view on this topic will be much different then. Trust me."

Erica swallowed her fear. She didn't want to be alone, yet somehow she was certain that she wouldn't be. If she waited to find a husband, it wouldn't hurt anything. She still wasn't in love with Alonzo. So she'd have to wait anyway.

"There you are." Veronica came strutting into the studio with some teal short shorts and a white halter top. Her stiletto heels clicked on the wooden floor as she neared them. Erica's eyes narrowed at the intrusion. Why did she have to come down and interrupt their conversation?

"Morning," Daddy responded.

Veronica went over and kissed him on the mouth. Erica turned away. It was too much for her to take. She readied herself to leave. "I'll talk to you later, Daddy."

"Was I interrupting something?" Veronica asked.

Lord, please don't let this woman bait me. *I don't think I'm strong enough to resist.* "We're finished," Erica said.

"I was discussing my daughter's options with her, explaining how important it is to grow up and start thinking about finding a man to marry," Daddy said.

Veronica turned to her. "Yes. I think marriage would be a good look for you. Don't you look forward to planning a wedding?"

"Not particularly. It's just another party."

Veronica laughed. "Not hardly. That's silly talk."

Erica's pulse quickened. "What's silly is marrying someone because you can't afford to take care of yourself. Then cheating on him every chance you get." *I knew I wasn't going to be able to keep that to myself.* This is the reason she was preparing to leave. Her mouth would not behave.

Veronica stared at her for a second as if she was trying to figure out what she meant. After it sunk in, she narrowed her eyes at Erica. All she needed was for Veronica to leap over and Erica would've body slammed her to the ground with no hesitation.

Erica's father interjected. "No one wants you to disrespect your vows. It's an opportunity to grow up and move away from the things you've been doing,"

Erica didn't want to talk about this anymore. Now that Cruella had entered the conversation, it was no longer worth having. She stared down Veronica before nodding at her father and turning to leave. At the very least, she had put Veronica on alert that she knew what was up. That should make her back off.

***

It seemed like Erica and Alonzo were on better terms already. Their previous night out was fun and uneventful for a change. She thought she would reward him with some lasagna. They were supposed to meet again later. Alonzo said he had a surprise for Erica. She was game. Erica would feed him and make sure she was prepared, wearing something he would like. She was looking forward to getting out of the house.

Erica was bent over the oven to check on the pasta when she heard footsteps behind her. She turned to see Veronica. She pretended she wasn't there.

"Hey. I need to talk to you," Veronica said.

"I don't have time. I'm busy."

"It won't take that long. It's urgent."

Erica closed the oven. "What do you want from me? I'm cooking for my man. Why can't you give me one day of peace in this house? I know you don't want me here, but I am here so it would be nice if you could let me exist on my side of the house and you can exist on your side." Erica unloaded on her pretty quickly. She didn't have patience for Cruella's games. So she really wanted to cut Veronica off before she got started.

Veronica stood next to her. "I want you to know I don't care what you think you have on me, you will never be able to get rid of me."

Erica leaned back and looked her up and down. "What are you talking about?" Veronica was definitely stupid enough to answer that question. So Erica decided to go ahead and ask.

"You know what I'm talking about. Don't ever even think about trying to come between me and your father. You got that?"

Erica burst into laughter.

"What the fuck are you laughing at?" Veronica sounded irritated.

That made Erica laugh even harder. She had to brace herself with one hand on the kitchen counter and the other holding her stomach.

"Oh, I can't help it. You're tripping." She started chuckling again.

Veronica shifted her weight back and forth. She looked like an animal who had been cornered and didn't know where to go. And Erica was enjoying every minute of it. Since she'd married her father, she made it her business to give Erica a hard time. She'd gotten worse in the last couple of years. Now, Erica had something on her. Something scandalous that could rip her world apart.

"You may think this is funny. If you start fucking with me, it will be no laughing matter. I assure you." Veronica stared at her intently.

"I know you don't think you're scaring me. I can take you with my eyes closed. You ain't shit." Erica moved closer. "Did you hear me? You ain't shit!" She pointed at Veronica. "So you watch yourself. You're a squatter in this family. Remember that."

With those words, Erica walked off around the counter. The lasagna had another fifteen minutes. Maybe Veronica would have moved along by then. The nerve of that heifer to step to her like she was going to do something. She was a whore and there was nothing she could do to clean it up. Daddy would find out about it. Her ass belonged to Erica now.

Chapter 21

Baby Doctor

Byron stared at his cellphone. *Daddy, I need to talk to you.* What could Erica have to talk to him about now? She probably wanted to stay longer or ask for money to leave. Or maybe she wanted his opinion on ole boy. He decided to stay out of that. He let his feelings be known to Alonzo. That was good enough for him. The rest had to be up to Erica or she would never grow up.

As the clock ticked through her two month deadline, he was also starting to think about her capacity to live on her own. She was young and young people make mistakes. She wasn't going to make it without his help. So he might as well resign himself to helping her. He wasn't going to tell her that yet. Byron realized that he was lost in thought when he heard the clicking of heels. Veronica appeared at the door of his pool room.

"We have company," she said.

"Now is not a good time." Byron moved to the other end of the table to prepare for a shot.

"Yes." She turned and walked out of the room.

Something told him he needed to follow her. He picked up his stick and shot one last time. Displeased with the way it turned out, he put the stick against the wall and went to see the visitor. He walked out into the foyer and saw a man in a gray suit and some glasses. He immediately offered his hand.

"This is Dr. Orum." She turned to the doctor. "This is my husband, Byron."

"Nice to meet you," the doctor said.

"Likewise. What brings you to these parts?" Byron put his hands on his waist.

"I'm a fertility doctor, and your wife invited me over to meet with you."

Byron felt like steam should be coming out of his ears like a cartoon. Who the fuck did she think she was to invite a fertility doctor? Wasn't nothing wrong with him. Period. "I'm sorry you came out for no reason. We are fine."

"Now, hold on." Veronica placed her hand on Byron's chest. "He's an expert, and given that we've been having some difficulties lately-"

Oh, no. She wasn't going there. Byron took a few steps closer to the door and opened it. "My apologies, Dr. Orum. We won't be needing your services."

"Byron!" Veronica put her hands on her hips. Byron didn't even see her. He would deal with her later.

Dr. Orum nodded. "I'm sorry for any misunderstanding. It was not my intention to impose or make anyone uncomfortable. I was under the impression that I was expected."

Byron smiled gently. "No problem." He continued to hold the door for the doctor.

The man stepped out. As soon as Byron closed the door, Veronica went in. "What the hell was that about?"

"Who the fuck do you think you are? Bringing him here?"

"Your wife."

"That's it and that's all. You have no right to do something like that."

"I have every right. How rude. We're supposed to be trying to have a baby. How are we supposed to do it now?"

"The natural way. If it happens, cool. If it doesn't, we'll have to live with it. Simple as that."

Veronica flipped her hair over her shoulder. "With all the technology in the world, that's a cruddy way to handle it."

"That's the way we're handling it!" Byron was losing his patience with Veronica. "I don't want to hear about it anymore."

She frowned. "Wait a minute."

"I said I'm done." Byron walked away. That was the end of discussion. He would not allow her to disrespect him that way. He didn't care if they ever had a baby. She'd better not pull that again.

***

"She's cheating, Daddy."

Byron frowned. "What are you talking about?"

"Veronica. I saw her."

"Erica . . . "

"I'm not lying. If you've never believed me before, you have to believe me now. I saw her. She's cheating."

He sighed. "With who?"

"The gardener."

A chuckle snuck out of him before he could stop it. There was no way his wife cheated on him with the lawn guy. "You know better than that."

"Look." Erica walked around her father's desk with her cell in her hand. "See. Right there."

Byron looked at the darkness on his daughter's screen. It didn't reveal anything. He wasn't even sure what it was. "What is that?"

"It's her and him." Erica pointed at the image, trying to show them. He still didn't see anything.

Byron pushed the phone away. "I don't want to look at anything else. This is nothing."

"No, it's not," Erica raised her voice. "Why don't you ever believe me?"

"Hush," Byron said. The last thing he needed was for her to get so hysterical that Veronica walked in and they got into a confrontation. "Sit down."

Erica reluctantly obeyed.

"It's clear that you two don't like each other. There's no reason to make things up."

Erica looked at the floor. She seemed hurt. It was unusual for her to look so rejected. It struck him. For a second, he wondered if he was rejecting her too quickly. Still, it seemed unlikely. His wife's taste was way too expensive for her to take up with a gardener.

"I can't believe you won't even consider it. She's no angel," Erica said.

"I'm not saying that she is. I just don't want you to resort to dirty tactics to make her angry. There's no need to do that."

"I'm not lying." Erica stood. "Before it's all over, you're gonna see it. You'll find out I'm telling the truth." She turned and left his office.

Byron sat back in his chair and watched her leave. He still wasn't totally convinced, but he knew his daughter well. She was *too* convinced. He wondered what was really going on.

Chapter 22

No Means No

Erica scowled as she turned the car unto the parking lot of an old restaurant. It was the kind that seniors would go to after church. There were a few cars scattered through the parking lot, but for the most part people had cleared out. It was probably their bed time. She parked under the light post. She kept the car on because she felt safer that way. She was only there to meet Leon, against her better judgement. She was not willing to stay long. Erica texted Leon on her phone.

Where are you?

She stared at the screen waiting for him to respond. Then there was a sharp knock on her window. She jumped, almost hitting her head on the roof of the car. Erica turned and saw Leon. She got out of the car, wanting to ring his neck.

"What the hell did you do that for?" she shouted.

"I was letting you know I was here."

"You could have texted me back."

"Why when I was right here?" Leon chuckled. "I'm sorry if I scared you."

Erica didn't find a damn thing funny. He was lucky she didn't knock him out. He appeared to realize how serious she was and stopped laughing.

"My bad. I'll text next time," he said.

"Whatever. You asked me to come here for what?" Erica asked.

"Do you want to go inside and get something to eat?" he asked.

"No. I want to know what this is about. I have some things to do."

"Like what?"

Like none of your business. "Stuff." Erica put her hands on her hips. "I don't want to eat. I want you to get to the point."

"How's your money holding up?" Leon asked.

She frowned. "It's fine."

"Do you have any left?"

"Why?"

"I could use some help." He placed one hand over the other.

She shrugged. "And?"

"Do you have any money you can give me?"

They'd been through this before. She couldn't believe he brought her all the way out there to hear the word "no." "I don't have any. I've been trying to get my stuff together."

"You're not done?"

"No." She squinted at him.

"I did you a favor. Now I need you to do me one."

"There's nothing I can do." She was on the edge with him. Erica wasn't going to be able to keep talking to him about what she couldn't do for him. In a minute, she was going to curse him out. "I have to have it to give it and I don't have it."

"I gave you the card. You have it. The bill says you've spent only about $1,500."

"Why did you open my mail?"

"Because it's at my house."

Erica heard his voice raise a few octaves. Was he really trying to get loud with her? Obviously, he didn't know her well. "It's still my mail. I asked you if you minded doing that for me. You asked me for money then, and I gave it to you. That's it."

"So that's it? You get what you want, and I'm in the wind?"

She shrugged. "I don't know what to tell you."

"You're just like you're father."

"What is that supposed to mean?"

"You don't care about anybody but yourself."

"It's not my job to take care of you. I gave you money for the favor you did. I don't have to keep giving you shit."

"What if I tell your daddy what you're doing behind his back?"

"Are you trying to threaten me?" Erica asked.

"I'm asking a question."

"What reason do you have to tell my dad unless you're starting trouble?"

"Trouble is when you open a credit card behind your parent's back."

"I don't need you to judge me because you can't take care of yourself. That's not my job."

"You don't think somebody needs to set you straight?"

"Are you crazy? How? Why?"

"About using your father?"

Erica turned back toward the car. "I'm done. Out of here. Good luck." As she got back into the car and closed her door, Leon leaned over the roof of the car.

"I'll give you twenty-four hours to change your mind. After that, I can't be held responsible for what happens."

Erica cranked up her car and drove away. She didn't know exactly what he was talking about. She would not let him intimidate her. He probably planned to tell her father, but he wouldn't believe him. Leon was going to have to find his own money.

Bottom line.

Chapter 23

You Did What?

It was clear to Byron that his wife was going to hold a grudge against him for treating the fertility doctor so cold. He had to nip this in the bud as soon as possible. So he had flowers delivered to the house for her. But he couldn't stop there. He made sure there was a pair of ten carat diamond earrings buried in the bouquet. When he heard the doorbell ring, he waited a few minutes before going outside to see her reaction. He caught her as she was closing the door behind the delivery guy.

Byron walked up to her with his hands in his pockets. She turned to see him approaching.

"Do you like it?" he asked.

Veronica shrugged. "Is this your way of apologizing?"

"Maybe."

She glanced at the flowers. "Maybe it'll work. Maybe it won't." She walked pass him toward the kitchen.

Byron shook his head. Veronica wasn't mad anymore. This was a game. She wanted to play up the incident to milk him for as much as she could. He followed behind her so that they could get this over with. He stood at the island while she put the flowers in the vase and filled it with water.

"What do you want?" he asked.

She continued to fuss with the flowers without answering him.

"I'm not gonna meet with a fertility doctor, especially at my house. As a matter of fact, I think you need to apologize for that."

Veronica turned and shot him an ice-cold stare.

"You don't agree?" Byron crossed his arms. Two could play this game.

She turned toward the window over the sink and put the flowers on the ledge.

"Both of us want what we want and we can both be stubborn. This is not a deal breaker. I need you to act with maturity and tell me what you'd like me to do."

Veronica turned to face him, crossing her arms as well. "I want a child. I shouldn't have to keep saying this."

"You don't. I do need you to take a different approach."

"And I need your support," she said.

"What would that look like?"

"Cooperation."

"Give me an example."

"Going to the doctor with me. Finding out what we need to do."

"Is that all?"

She rolled her eyes. "Well, that's not all."

"I mean in terms of support."

"It's a start."

Byron would not be able to get out of this. He was going to have to go along in order to get any peace in the house. He ran his hands over his face. "Fine. Make the appointment. I will be there."

"You promise?" Veronica stared at him with wary eyes.

He sighed. "Yes."

She walked to him and hugged him. Byron was still holding on to the idea that they couldn't have kids. They didn't need them. Then a thought hit him. What if she was cheating on him? Their prenup would prevent her from getting any spousal support if it were proven that she strayed during the marriage, but a baby would be a whole other situation. He would have to pay at least $15,000 per month. He stood straight as a board at the prospect. Veronica noticed and pulled away from him.

"What's wrong?" she asked.

Byron shook his head. "Nothing. I had a sharp pain in my back."

"Oh? Where?" She moved around him to find the source of his discomfort.

He pointed to the left side of his lower back. She applied pressure. "Does this hurt?"

"No."

"What about this?" she asked as she pushed her fingers against his skin again.

He shook his head. "No. I think it's gone."

"Well, we need to keep an eye on it." She rubbed his back before walking away.

Byron watched her for a few seconds before walking over to the counter where he spotted some mail. He found an envelope addressed to him. There was no sender information listed. He opened it and found a note with a bill.

Mr. Mercy,

This is a bill from a credit card in your name. I know you didn't open it. So I thought you should know what your daughter is up to.

Sincerely,

Looking out for you

Byron looked at the bill for almost $2,000. His nostrils flared. Surely, Erica knew better than to open a card without his permission. He went searching through the house for her. He ran into Lana dusting in the living room.

"Have you seen Erica?" he asked.

"I believe she's in the guesthouse."

He dashed toward the side of the main house to find her. Byron saw Erica as soon as he opened the door to the house. She was sitting on the couch with her foot on the table, painting her toe nails. He spotted a few bags in the corner. Erica looked at him startled.

"Daddy, what are you doing here?"

"It's my house," he said.

"Yeah, but usually you don't come in here."

He stepped into the living room. "Are you hiding something from me?"

"No, this is my only spot to get away from Cruella. What's wrong? You look funny."

"Where did you get all this stuff?" he asked.

She glanced over to the bags. "From the store."

"How did you pay for it?"

She paused. "A card."

"Which one?" Byron could already see the wheels turning in Erica's brain. She was figuring out what to say. If she lied, it would take everything in him not to slap her across her mouth. Instead, she remained silent.

"I want an answer, Erica."

"I don't remember," she mumbled.

"Could it be this one?" Byron showed her the bill from his newly discovered card.

Erica's eyes grew big. Her chest rose as she breathed faster. She opened her mouth to speak and closed it right away.

"You don't have anything to say?"

She swallowed and screwed the top on the nail polish bottle.

Byron nodded. "I have something to say. I want you out ASAP."

She gasped.

He held his hand up. "I don't wanna hear it. I have no more lectures for you. It's time for you to leave. I want you out of here by tomorrow." Byron threw the bill at her and turned to leave the house. This time, he would not budge. Erica had to go.

Chapter 24

Moving In

Erica had nowhere else to go. She supposed she felt lucky to have Alonzo. She never thought she'd find herself saying that. Unfortunately, it didn't cheer her up.

She sat on his bed, overlooking the city lights in his high rise apartment. Alonzo walked over and sat next to her. He offered her a drink. She shook her head.

"C'mon. It might help." He pushed the drink back in front of her.

This time, she took it. Erica sipped gingerly. After she swallowed a few times, Alonzo seemed satisfied and he turned to down his own drink.

After savoring his drink, he faced her again. "Have you talked to your dad since you got here?"

Erica shook her head. She didn't have much to say to her father. Making her leave was unforgiveable.

"When do you plan to let him know you're here?"

She shrugged. "It doesn't matter."

"Why?"

"Because he's the one who told me to leave." Those words tasted bitter. She bent over as if someone had stabbed her in the stomach.

"He would still want to know that you're safe."

She really didn't want to hear that right now. She downed the rest of her drink, which turned out to be chardonnay.

"It'll work out. You two will make amends."

Erica put the glass on his nightstand and stared back out at the street lights. She felt trapped. No matter what she did, she couldn't get ahead. A tear gathered in her eye and spilled over. She wiped it away.

Despite her attempt to keep her sadness unnoticed, Alonzo saw it.

"Hey." He put his arm around her and pulled her close.

Erica tried to resist. She was in no condition to do so—she couldn't tell if it was due to her emotions or the alcohol. Alonzo won out, pulling her in for a bear hug. More tears followed while he held on to her. He rubbed her shoulder until her tears subsided. When she looked at him, he leaned in to kiss her. She reluctantly returned the kiss. Her subtle resistance didn't seem to be a deterrent.

He reached into her shirt and began massaging her left breast. His hand felt good. His lips roamed down her neck. He flicked his tongue over her skin. She shivered. He took that as an invitation to start undressing her. She helped him remove her wrapped blouse. He marveled at her exposed breasts, clearly his favorite part of her body. He threw his clothes off, and they went on for several minutes with the night sky in the background.

Alonzo and Erica lay down next to each other on the floor, still nude. She rested her head on his chest, listening to his heart beat settle. It helped calm her. She still wasn't in love with him, but he was helping her through this difficult time.

"Do you really want to move away from here?" Alonzo asked.

Erica thought about it. "It would be better than being at everyone's mercy."

"What if I could change that?"

She glanced at him. "Huh?"

Alonzo leaned over and reached for something. He handed her a little box. "Open it."

Erica looked at him and frowned. He nodded. She reluctantly opened the box to find one of the biggest diamond rings she'd ever seen, and that was saying a lot. She yelped.

"I know you're looking for some big adventure. Love can be an adventure too. You know? I want to be your adventure. I want to make you free."

Erica's mouth dropped.

"Will you marry me?" he asked.

"Are you serious?"

"What?"

Erica sat up. "But our time isn't up yet." He was supposed to be giving her two months.

"Well, we're already living together. What's the wait?"

She frowned and stared at the floor.

Alonzo's shoulders tensed. "I take it you're not happy."

"I thought we were having fun."

"We are. How long do you want to have fun?"

"As long as possible."

He snapped the ring box shut and stood up from the floor. She could sense his anger and hurt. She was surprised. Why did he want to marry her? It's probably the one thing she didn't dream about growing up. "I'm sorry," she said, half-heartedly.

Alonzo's back was facing her, the moonlight spotlighting his tight behind. "For what?"

Erica stood, feeling the need to make nice. She walked up behind him. "Being insensitive. I don't mean to upset you."

"It's no problem." His head was down.

"I don't understand. Why do you need to get married now? I've never seen a happily married couple. Have you?"

He faced her with narrowed eyes. Erica backed away from him. Flashes of the car incident crossed her mind.

"Don't play games with me. I'm not gonna be your fool."

"What are you talking about?"

"You're not gonna stay here and use me like you did your father. Get it together or you can find another place to live."

Chapter 25

Change of Plans

fter his call from Alonzo, Byron hung up his phone. He shouldn't have been shocked. Erica never could do things for herself. Why wouldn't she run to him? Byron had mixed feelings about it, though. On one hand, he was relieved that she was finally out of the house. A chance to learn how to survive. On another, Byron saw it as his daughter making more poor choices. She always jumped into something without much thought. Then she looked for him to bail her out. She refused to stand on her own two feet. He didn't intend to save her this time. He planned to let her finally learn from her mistakes. A hard decision.

Byron stared out the window of his office, contemplating the news he'd heard when he saw Veronica outside chatting with Jose, the gardener.

Byron narrowed his eyes. This wasn't unusual. Still there was something about their interaction that seemed . . . overly familiar. Maybe it was the way she looked at him. Perhaps it was the way she touched his arm when she laughed.

He wanted answers. So he walked briskly downstairs. When he went outside, Veronica continued to talk, unaware that he was approaching. Jose saw him and stopped smiling, instead turning back to the lawn tools at his feet. Veronica looked over her shoulder and spotted Byron.

"That'll be all, Jose." Veronica shooed the young man.

Jose scurried away. Veronica had recovered so quickly the average person wouldn't have noticed, but he'd seen her converse with Jose and knew that it was an act. Veronica changed to an expression of concern as she scrutinized Byron's face.

"What's wrong?"

"Erica is with Alonzo," Byron said, choosing a different subject.

"Good."

Byron sighed.

"This is great. She's out of your hair now. Why are you so concerned?"

"He's not a good guy."

"That's for her to figure out. I think you want to control her life. She's happy."

"How would you know?"

"A woman is always happy when she finds a man who will take care of her."

Those words struck Byron like a fist to his stomach. Of course. That's how he was to Veronica. Security. He knew she was savvy and wanted the best, but he must have started to believe that they at least had a real marriage. Shame on him. *Get some control, Byron.*

Veronica stared at him with an expectant look on her face. She was waiting for him to respond.

"That doesn't mean she's happy. It means she's using him." Byron turned to go back into the house. He could hear Veronica following him.

"Enough about Erica already. It's time to talk about our plans." She caught up to him. "I made an appointment today."

"Where?" Byron asked.

"The doctor. Remember? I make the appointment and you'll show up."

"Oh. Now?"

"Yes. What other time is there?" Veronica continued to follow him into the living room.

He sat on the couch. "This is bad timing."

Veronica placed her hands on her hips. "How? You don't have anything to do."

"I have some other things on my mind. I can't absorb what some doctor is saying right now."

"Is this about Erica? She's gone. Get over it."

"Listen." Byron raised his voice and injected twice the usual amount of bass to it. "I don't have time for that right now."

Veronica shrieked. "You snake. How could you lie to me? I asked you what you wanted and I set it up just for you to let me down. I can't believe you."

No matter what she said, he would not change his mind. There would be no plans to start having a baby until he got down to the bottom of her true motives. This whole thing wasn't sitting right with him.

"I don't know what to say," Byron said.

"You're an asshole." Veronica stomped off.

He could hear the sound of her feet hitting the stairs hard with each step. He leaned back on the couch. Byron had been too easy on her. Too soft. He'd given her whatever she wanted, and he was certain she was taking advantage of that. He would fix it. He was going to locate a private investigator to get down to the bottom of this. He wanted to know what was going on and how long it was going on. He would need it in case something should happen. Like a divorce.

***

Byron sat on the bench in Watershed Park. There were kids outside playing. He watched them and wondered if he would want to experience dealing with that again. If he were honest with himself, he would acknowledge that he never dealt with it the first time. When Erica was a child, he was gone a lot. His sister, Angie, had raised her off and on until she was about twelve or thirteen. That's why it was always so weird that they didn't get along. He would think they would be closer. That was not the case. He even thought she would be relieved that Angie took the baby. Instead, Erica was even more resentful. Byron didn't know how to explain it.

Before he could think about it too much, Patrick, the private eye he'd been referred to, walked toward him. He had a neat mustache and relaxed suit. He sat on the bench. As Byron requested, he was careful not to sit too close. Yet he was close enough that they could talk without shouting. The man pulled out his cell phone and began staring at it intently. Byron pulled out his book and opened to chapter five.

"Glad we could meet," Patrick said.

"Same here," Byron said, staring at his book.

"Where did you want to start?"

"Not sure. I've never used one of these before," Byron said.

"People hire one all the time. It's the best way to get the answer to unanswered questions."

"That's exactly what I need. To know what's going on." Byron paused. "There are some issues in my family . . ."

"Say no more. That's what I'm here for. I assure you I'm professional. I don't use any shady or unethical practices to obtain information.

"I don't care if you do. I just need answers."

Patrick cleared his throat. "Who do you want me to follow?"

"I want you to follow two people."

"Um. Why two?"

"Well, they are both acting strange and it's for different reasons."

"Who?"

"My wife and my daughter's boyfriend."

"I don't usually do two at a time."

"That's what I need."

"It will definitely cost you extra."

"Money's not an issue."

Patrick nodded. "Very well, then."

"I heard that you're discreet," Byron stated.

"Very. I go unnoticed and keep the client anonymous as well."

"That's what I like to hear."

"What is it you're looking for exactly?"

Byron sighed. "I'm in a sticky situation with my wife, and I want to make sure that everything is kosher."

"I see," Patrick nodded. A smile pulled at the corner of his mouth. "Would this have anything to do with infidelity?"

Byron tightened his lips and narrowed his eyes at the book in front of him.

"Listen," Patrick said. "That's the most common reason people hire me. I'm used to that, and I take care to make sure I get down to the truth in a way that leaves my clients' dignity intact."

This Patrick fellow was saying all the right words. It was putting Byron at ease somewhat, but he was still uncomfortable with having to do this at all.

"What about the other subject?" Patrick asked.

"I don't trust him. He's taken up with my daughter, and I don't think he means her well."

"Let me guess. You're not able to tell her that, right?"

"It's complicated."

Patrick nodded. "How old is your daughter?"

"She's twenty-one."

"Still over protective?"

"No, I not only have to protect her. I have to protect the security I've built." Byron rubbed his chest. "I feel like I'm getting attacked at all sides. I need to get down to the bottom of this."

Patrick nodded. "I'll have the answers to your questions within a couple of weeks."

Chapter 26

Pregnant

S aturday morning, Erica woke up, rolled over and downed a quick swig of Vodka. She rubbed her stomach. She'd been feeling sick and she wasn't sure why. She did know one thing: she was not prepared for marriage. At the same time, she felt like she needed her time with Alonzo, even if it was only going to be a pit stop before moving to her own place. Erica was trying to keep things level while she worked on getting her life together. She wasn't sure how much longer she would be able to keep him from issuing an ultimatum.

Despite feeling sick, Erica managed to stumble into the kitchen, where Alonzo was scanning his phone and drinking coffee. He looked up when he saw her.

"You look terrible," he said.

“Thanks.”

“Seriously. You should see a doctor.”

“No, thank you.”

“I can go with you, if you’re afraid.”

“I’m not afraid of anything.”

“Then why won’t you go?”

“Because I’m fine.”

“No, you’re not.”

This was annoying. “What do you know?”

“I know a sick person when I see ‘em.”

She opened the refrigerator. “I don’t need no doctor.”

Alonzo stood and walked to her as she closed the refrigerator. She opened the bottle of orange juice and poured a little bit of it into a glass before reaching for another bottle of vodka to pour in it.

“If you keep that up, you’re gonna need AA instead of a doctor.”

“Is that right?” she asked before taking a swig.

“Yep.”

"Get outta here with that." Erica waved him off and took her drink back into the bedroom. She took a few more swigs and lay back under the warm covers to fall asleep. A few hours later, she was awakened by a sharp pain in her back. It startled her and made her lie straight as a board. She reached for her night stand and knocked her glass of Vodka and juice to the floor.

"Alonzo! Alonzo!"

She didn't hear anything. She didn't know where he was and if he would be around to hear her call. She wanted to cry. She called for him again. Then he came dragging into the room.

"What?" he asked.

"I need help."

Alonzo took one look at her and sprang into action. He picked her up and drove her to the nearest hospital. The nurse ushered her into a room and proceeded to ask her questions.

"What are you experiencing today?"

"Pains in my back," Erica said, weakly.

The nurse pulled out the instrument to check her blood pressure. She squeezed the ball. "Blood pressure is high." She went over to the chart and began writing. "When was your last menstrual?"

Erica looked at the ceiling. "I can't remember."

"Was it a couple of weeks ago?"

"I think so. I'm not sure."

The nurse wrote that down. Erica was sent to the back where she underwent a series of tests, including a blood test and pelvic exam. She lay in the hospital bed, staring up at the dull lights alone. The last time she was here was when she gave birth to the baby. This was such a sad place.

She wondered what was wrong with her. She hoped it wasn't fatal. She had so much more to do. She really hadn't accomplished anything and that was a shame. She closed her eyes. *God, I know I haven't been the best person in the world. If you help me through this I'm going to try to do the right thing.* Alonzo walked through the door, interrupting her prayer.

"Did they give you something for the pain?" he asked.

"Yes."

He nodded. The doctor walked in a few seconds behind him.

"Hello, Erica. I'm Dr. Pembrook. I'll be working with you today." He flipped open her folder. "So you had some back pains?"

Erica nodded.

"Lower back or upper back?"

"Lower."

He nodded and placed the folder on the nearby counter. He pressed against her back to determine the point of pain. When she flinched, he backed up and sat on a stool next to her bed. "The pressure you're feeling on your back will subside soon. Did you know you were pregnant?"

Erica tried to sit up. "What are you talking about?"

"You're about three weeks along."

"What?" Alonzo asked.

"Don't worry. Everything is fine," the doctor said to Erica. "You're going to be fine. Since you've had a baby before, I don't see there being any problems with this pregnancy."

Alonzo's forehead wrinkled. "Wait."

Erica could feel Alonzo looking at her. She avoided his glare. She had a lot on her mind and didn't need his judgments.

"When?" Alonzo asked.

Dr. Pembrook stammered. "I'm sorry. Is there something wrong?"

Big mouth doctor.

"When was this pregnancy?" Alonzo barked.

The doctor cleared his throat. "I'm going to put in a prescription for you. I'll give you two a minute to talk." Dr. Pembrook carefully exited the room.

"You were pregnant? When?" Alonzo started in before the door could even close good.

Erica scowled. "It doesn't matter."

"Like hell it doesn't."

"I don't have to listen to you talk to me like this."

"What the fuck is going on?"

"It was a long time ago."

"Have you ever been married?"

"No."

"Then who is the father?"

"That's none of your business," she snapped.

"Excuse me?"

"You heard me. Now if all you're going to do is talk to me crazy, you can leave my room." Erica turned away from him on her side. This was not the time or place to explore her sordid past.

She could hear him huff. "This isn't over."

She didn't care how mad he was. She would never tell him about the hidden baby. She meant what she said. It truly wasn't his business.

Chapter 27

Tell Me the Truth

Byron should have known this would happen. He shook his shoulders and adjusted his hand position to try and get a better grip on the golf club, but he was distracted by the news he'd received from Erica. He shouldn't be surprised, but after all the disappointments his daughter gave him, he'd hoped she would hold off on having more babies. He hated the fact that he was disappointed in her again. And it hurt. She was still his child. He took a few practice swings before lining the club up to the ball, forcing himself to concentrate. Before he could take a good swing, Alonzo stomped toward him.

"Why didn't you tell me she had a baby?"

Byron stopped in mid swing. Who was he talking to? He didn't care that Alonzo was angry when he found out about the other child. He was lucky Byron didn't thump him back out of Florida. Byron didn't appreciate him running into his house demanding things from him.

"What the hell is your problem?"

"Erica is pregnant. I know this isn't her first time. What happened to the other baby?" Alonzo stood there expectantly.

Byron stared back at him, willing himself to keep his hands to his sides.

Alonzo jumped his way. "Why didn't you tell me?"

Byron changed his grip on the golf club so that it could be used as a weapon. "Boy, you better sit your ass down. Who are you barking at?"

Alonzo stalled. Once Byron shot him a no-nonsense stare, he eased down in a nearby chair.

"First, we need to talk about *you* impregnating my daughter and what *you're* gonna do about it."

"I was always trying to do the right thing. I asked her to marry me. She declined," Alonzo said. "Now, I'm not even sure I want to."

"What is that supposed to mean?"

"I don't want a woman who would lie to me."

"She didn't lie."

"She didn't tell the truth. I can't trust a woman like that."

This wasn't the ideal situation. Byron had changed his opinion about Alonzo and no longer thought he was the greatest match for Erica. Now that there was another baby on the way, he couldn't bare having another child in the family born illegitimately due to Erica's reckless behavior. The embarrassment would be too much. He also couldn't imagine her moving back home with him and Veronica. They would kill each other. There was only one thing to do. "Then you have to change her mind."

"You still haven't answered my question."

"It's not pertinent."

"To who?"

"Anybody, especially not you. It was a while back. It's settled. It's over."

"How long ago? What happened to the baby? Who is the father?"

"I understand this is a shock to you. It would be to most people, but you're making a big deal out of nothing. There's nothing you need to know. It's water under the bridge."

"Are you saying you're not gonna tell me?"

Byron deepened his voice. "I'm telling you to go home and take care of my daughter. Now." The sternness in Byron's voice made it crystal clear that he wasn't going to listen to much more. Alonzo seemed to sense he wasn't going to get any farther with Byron. Without a word, he stood and stomped back out the door.

Veronica walked in the room after he left. "What was all that about?"

Byron tossed his golf club to the ground. "Erica is pregnant."

She straightened her back. "Oh."

He nodded. "And he found out about the other one."

Her jaw dropped. "Oh."

"He wanted details about it. You know, when it happened."

"And who's the father." Veronica finished.

Byron sat in a chair and looked at his rolling, green acres of land without responding to Veronica.

"It doesn't bother you that you still don't know who the father is?" she pressed.

"It doesn't matter." It really didn't, but secretly he would always wonder. Not that he wanted to meet the man who impregnated Erica and left her to figure it out on her own. He'd hurt him if they met. He only wanted a better understanding of his daughter. There was a big part of her he didn't know. It didn't nag him, but he couldn't help wondering about it sometimes. Who was he kidding? It was probably better that he not know. It may be more than he could handle. Like the whole Leon situation. Surely, there were things about him that she couldn't handle.

Veronica sat across from him and swung her hair behind her shoulders. "What about us?"

He looked at her.

"Our baby." She smiled.

He was suddenly reminded of his investigation of her. Any day now he should be getting some feedback on it. Until then he needed to keep her baby aspirations at bay. Stall her. "What baby?"

"Don't play games now. You promised me we would work on it." Veronica started to shake and clinch her hands in a fist.

Byron sighed. "You're right. I did. Given these new developments, I need to keep my eye on that. Nobody's even supposed to know about the other baby and now we have a new one on the way. I knew Erica wasn't going to do the right thing."

"What does that have to do with us? You always use her as an excuse."

"You're overreacting."

"And you let your daughter ruin everything." Veronica shot up from her seat and stomped off.

That went over well. He was willing to take this lump. Byron couldn't make another move until he figured out what was going on in his own home.

Chapter 28

Accepted

Alonzo and Erica hadn't been talking much since they found out she was pregnant. He was especially pensive about finding out that she'd had a baby before. Erica was dead set against explaining her prior situation. She didn't even want to think about it. Despite their distance, Alonzo suddenly came up to her and asked her to go on a boat ride. It was the first olive branch he had extended since the baby news. So she obliged.

A chef prepared their dinner. They coasted along the water, watching the moonlight bounce its light off the river. The moon looked particularly big where they were. She figured now was as good a time as any to approach him about marriage.

"It's a great night to be out here," she said.

"It is. You want anything to drink?" he asked.

She frowned. "You know I can't drink."

"I'm not talking about alcohol. We have juice and soda," Alonzo said.

"Oh." Erica's gaze dropped to the floor. "I'll have juice."

He poured her some into a glass and handed it to her. It felt empty. Erica looked at it, wishing it were alcohol, but she understood she had to be responsible now. Alonzo poured himself a glass.

She glanced at him. "Thank you for everything."

He stopped short before taking a sip. "You're welcome."

"Seriously. You've been great," she said.

He looked around. "What's going on? You can't break up with me. We're having a kid."

"I know. That's not what I meant."

He nodded. "Oh. Glad to hear it. You scared me for a minute."

"No need to be scared. I wanted to let you know I appreciate you."

"Well, thank you." Alonzo touched her hand and drew it back as if it were hot. "We're going to be a real family soon. We have to plan for the future."

Whether she liked it or not, he was right. It seemed like she would have some support and it was a good thing because she needed it. Maybe it would be easier to handle this one. As she thought about the new child, guilt seeped into her mind about the first one. She had already proven to be a bad mother, not much better than her own—which was a hard pill to swallow. Growing up, Erica told herself that she would not abandon her children the way her mother did her. She had failed.

Alonzo put his arms around her as if he sensed that she needed comfort. "Have you given any more thought to getting married?"

She switched her weight from her left to her right foot. "I guess."

"And?"

Erica bit her lip. "I don't know."

"We have to do something. The child is coming, and we need to make a home for it. We can start by turning our union into a legitimate legal partnership."

As she thought about his suggestion, that seemed the only option now. Before she was fighting to stay, and now he was adamant she stay and they get married. The thought slightly bored her, but it wasn't about her anymore. She would need his support in the upcoming months.

"What are your biggest concerns about marrying me?"

She shook her head. She wasn't ready for this life commitment, but at this point what choice did she have? There was nothing else to do. Nowhere else to turn. Her daddy didn't even want her back in the house.

Alonzo pulled out a small box and opened it. A four carat diamond ring sat pretty against the blue velvet. "Are you ready to marry me now?"

The ring got a small smile out of Erica. She held out her hand, fingers stretched out in a fan. Alonzo put the ring on her wedding finger. He hugged her and they looked back out at the water.

Erica could have cried. She felt like her life was ending instead of beginning. She was having another child unplanned and she was marrying a man she was certain she wasn't in love with. She took a deep breath and closed her eyes, hoping to stop the wave of emotion threatening to rise to the surface.

"Are you happy?" Alonzo asked.

Erica nodded. "Yes."

"Before we get married, is there anything else I need to know about you?"

She sighed. "No."

"When are you going to tell me about the other kid? Did it die?"

"I don't want to talk about it."

Chapter 29

Big Argument

Erica walked up to the steps of her father's house. She hadn't been gone that long. Yet it still felt unfamiliar. This was the first time she spent away from the house. It had always been her home. It felt strange going there as a guest. She wished she could click her heels and live there again. Life was simpler, even though she had so many crises there. It was a time when her father loved her. Now she wasn't so sure. He made her move out. Who does that to someone they love? That's what she asked herself as she walked into her father's office.

Daddy looked up from his desk.

"We're early," she said, as she moved closer to his desk. She'd left Alonzo in the living room.

"I see," was all Daddy said.

"What is this thing about anyway?" she asked.

"We need to talk about the future." As her father spoke, he happened to glance at her finger. He'd spotted the rock on her left hand, engagement finger. A feeling of foreboding hit Erica. There was no sign of approval or happiness in his expression. "I see I'm not the only one thinking about the future."

Erica followed his gaze. "No. Aren't you happy? I'm doing what you want."

She resented his coolness toward the new developments. She didn't come there to be treated like her situation didn't matter. This was major. She could use his support.

He raised an eyebrow. "This isn't the happiest occasion. It's about doing the right thing."

"That's all that matters to you. Making everything right and perfect," Erica said.

"What matters is that we handle this responsibly."

For a few seconds, silence hung in the air. Erica's feelings of resentment gave way to a moment of guilt. "I'm sorry, Daddy."

He didn't respond.

"I am. I shouldn't have gotten the card without your consent. I didn't know what to do. You were putting me out with no money."

"You don't have to worry about that anymore. Alonzo can take care of you and the child. All's well," he said.

Erica narrowed her eyes. She didn't believe him, but decided not to talk about it any farther. Her emotions were in danger of getting out of control. "How did you know about the card anyway?"

"Someone sent me the information."

She was certain Leon sent it to him. All she said was, "Oh."

"When is the wedding date?" Daddy asked.

"Huh? Oh, um. I was thinking two weeks from now."

He frowned. "Why so soon? That doesn't leave any time for planning."

"I don't need much. I shouldn't be waiting too long anyway—with the baby and all." Erica glanced at her stomach. She couldn't believe she was doing this again. And so soon. She really didn't want to make a fuss. "Listen. I know we haven't been on the best of terms, but I wanted to ask you if I could have it here. In the backyard. There won't be a lot of people—"

"Sure. No problem."

Erica's mouth dropped open. She didn't have to beg. Lana came in to inform them that dinner was ready. Erica and Daddy migrated to the dining room, where Alonzo was already waiting. He reached out his hand to her father, and the two men shook hands. Alonzo stuck out his chest. Though he proposed to Erica, she could tell that he still didn't appreciate the fact that she had a baby from someone else. He probably thought something special had been taken away from him. If he only knew how unremarkable the situation was.

When everybody sat, they dined on filet mignon with champagne and a side of cake for dessert. Of course, Erica avoided the alcohol as required. She also remained relatively quiet as the night drew on. She was uninspired to keep up the appearance of phoniness. Instead, she sat and rolled her eyes while Alonzo and Veronica bantered back and forth in a half joking, half flirting manner. Veronica would take any opportunity to get under Erica's skin. She was pathetic. And to think, Daddy still didn't believe she was cheating on him. Daddy hit a glass with his fork. All the random chatter stopped.

He stood. "Thank you all for coming out. I know you could have been anywhere else. I'm glad you chose to spend it here. That lets me know you value family as much as I do. As we know, there will be a new edition to our family soon." He looked around the table. Veronica took a swig of champagne. "It's my hope that we can put any differences we've had aside and focus on this new responsibility. This new life. He or she deserves for us to give them the utmost respect."

Everyone remained quiet. That's it? What was this supposed to do? If he was trying to make Veronica act right, it wasn't going to happen.

"I thank you for that," Alonzo said. "It means a lot to me that you accept this baby. We are all family, and I look forward to starting my life with Erica." He beamed at Erica and rubbed her hand. She tensed a little. Veronica raised her glass. "To family."

"To family," they all said in unison, clinking glasses.

Once the dinner was over, Alonzo wanted to linger around the house.

"I think we should go now," Erica whispered into his ear.

"A little longer," he said, patting her on the butt.

"Thanks for dinner," Alonzo said to her father as he entered the kitchen.

"It's the least I can do for my first grandchild," Daddy said.

Everybody in the room, including Erica, stopped and stared at him. Why did he have to say that? Another reason for them to have to ignore the elephant in the room. She felt the need to rush in and cover it up.

"Well, thank you, Daddy."

Veronica sucked her teeth. Unfortunately, Erica heard it.

"Is there a problem?"

"You act like your father is the only one who does anything around here."

"Isn't he?" Erica asked.

"No. You're so disrespectful. You've always been a spoiled brat." Veronica slurred her words.

"I guess that makes two of us then, huh?" Erica shot back.

"I'm not a spoiled brat. I'm a wife. I deserve everything I have."

"Right." Erica mocked.

"Just because you don't like it doesn't mean I should apologize for it. I live a good life. Get yours."

Erica held up her right hand. "Wait a minute. Who are you talking to?"

Veronica turned to walk over to Erica. "You, bitch."

"Whoa. Hold on. Let's all calm down." Alonzo stepped between the two women.

Veronica pointed at Alonzo. "You calm down. She's a triflin' hoe."

Erica had enough of her. "Keep talking. You sound jealous to me. What is it? Is it my man? Is it my clothes? I know. It's my baby. That's right. You can't have one."

"Shut up," Veronica shouted.

"Better luck next life time," Erica mocked. "If you're nice to me, I might let you hold it."

"You know what? Fuck you. And all of your kids."

"This is getting out of hand. Why don't we all call it a night?" Alonzo said. He stood between Erica and Veronica, his hands in front of his fiancé.

How ironic. Now he wanted to leave. He was going to have to start listening to her if they were going to be married.

"That's right. She can take her ass somewhere else. If she got a problem with me, the door is that way." Veronica pointed toward the front door.

Erica stretched over Alonzo's shoulder. "Because I know you're drunk, I'm gonna let you live."

"I wish you would try me." Veronica took off her shoes.

Erica looked at Alonzo. "Is she crazy?"

"Jump over here, and I'll show you how crazy I am."

"Veronica! Cut it out," Daddy said. However, she didn't even look at him. He grabbed her shoulders and shook her. "Stop it."

She shook herself loose. "Let go of me. If you want to protect her, that's your problem. I'm not gonna do it anymore."

Erica's father frowned. "You're overreacting."

Veronica sniffed. "She's disgusting. And you're disgusting if you keep protecting her. She's nothing but a slut. A filthy one, at that."

"Why are you worried about me?"

Alonzo grabbed Erica's arm as she leaned forward.

"I would never worry about filth like you. What kind of woman gives up her baby then gets pregnant again to keep that one? You're scum. Pure dirt."

"That's enough." Daddy shouted at Veronica. "Stop this nonsense and go upstairs." His eyes bore into hers.

"You're the dirty one. Standing here spreading bullshit about me," Erica chided.

"Yeah, right."

Alonzo and Erica's father held the two women apart. Erica was trying to edge closer so that she could touch Veronica.

"Erica, it's time to go," Daddy warned.

The two women were still arguing over the men's shoulders and trying to get to each other.

"She needs to get her nasty ass out of my house."

"You can't kick me out of my daddy's house." Erica pushed over Alonzo to try and get to Veronica.

"I said get out! You don't belong here." She tried to run for Erica, but she was caught and dragged toward the stairs.

Alonzo picked Erica up and took her out of the house, kicking and screaming. He finally got Erica out the door and into the car. Why did he have to keep her from beating her? That was all she needed. One of these days, Veronica was going to get hers, and Erica would be the one to give it to her.

Chapter 30

Wedding on Deck

Veronica tossed clothes from her closet onto the bed. She did it with such ferociousness that some of the clothes fell off the bed and onto the floor. She had beat Byron into the room and he leaned against the door frame to watch her go crazy. She started to mumble.

"What was that?" he asked.

"Leave me alone. I'm sick of this. I have to go."

Byron crossed his arms. "Where?"

She stopped before throwing a blouse. "Away from here. I can't stand this anymore. You can stay here with your daughter, allowing her to do whatever she wants. I'm out."

"Erica doesn't even live here anymore and you're the one who started this."

"Excuse me?"

"Don't play stupid. What is it with you, anyway?"

Veronica's mouth dropped. "Me?"

"Yeah, you're hatred for Erica is over the top. Makes me wonder what's really behind it." Byron wondered if she was going to take the bait and admit that she'd done things she shouldn't have. For a split second, he could tell she was thinking about her deeds. Then she quickly erased any trace of remorse from her made-up features.

"You have it wrong. She's the one who hates me. She's treated me like crap ever since we met, and all you did was turn a blind eye. Well, I'm tired of it." Veronica turned back around and continued pulling clothes out of the closet. "And I'm taking all of my stuff with me."

Byron could see that he had to remind her who she was and who he was. "Fine. Leave . . .you need to leave the clothes here, though."

"What?"

"And the watches, earrings, necklaces and rings. Don't even think about leaving here in my car."

She stopped and stared at him with horror in her eyes. "That's my car."

"No, it's not. I bought it. Just like everything else. Or did you forget?"

"I'm your wife, and you gave it to me. Therefore it's mine."

"Not according to our prenup. You can leave but take nothing with you."

Byron watched Veronica go from anger and arrogance to disbelief and humility. She didn't have the power she thought she had. If she wanted to continue with this foolishness, she would learn the hard way. The investigator's upcoming report would give him all the ammunition he would need to keep her from getting all of his money. He was the one in the power position. If Veronica thought she would leave and use his money to support her lifestyle with another man, she was really delusional. All she had was her looks and one day, that would fade.

She narrowed her eyes. "You don't own me."

"Then leave," he said. Byron stared at her as her feet remained stuck to the floor. She wasn't going anywhere. Like Erica, the only place she could go was to another man's house, and, from her choice for a side piece, she was truly out of gas.

"That's what I thought," Byron walked out the door and shouted over his shoulder, "Now clean that shit up."

***

Veronica had been avoiding Byron since their argument. He was enjoying the peace. At least she wasn't asking him for something, like a baby. This gave him time to work on Erica's wedding.

It was funny. Usually, women can't wait to plan their wedding. When Byron married Veronica, everything had to be her way. That was not the case with his daughter. She virtually didn't care. The only thing she cared about was the dress. She had to have control over the dress. Other than that, she didn't care what the wedding looked like, which made it easy. Even though she didn't care, he wasn't going to allow the wedding to look shabby. He intended to invite his social circle for networking purposes. Therefore it would still be an important affair. Extravagant but elegant. He hired a wedding planner to put it together. The best to be exact. All he needed was for his family to behave themselves on the big day. As the wedding planner, Elisabeth, sat across from him at the conference table, he faded in and out of the details that she gave him. He was about as uninterested as Erica. Byron wanted the planner to do the job without telling him about it.

"Is there anything you want to tell me about the bride? Her preferences?" Elisabeth asked.

"No."

"What are her colors?"

"She doesn't have any colors."

"What?"

"The only thing she's decided on is a dress. She's not too interested in the rest of the details. That's why you're here." Byron shot her a fake smile. It didn't seem to do anything to instill confidence in her.

"I need something to work with. This is like working from scratch."

"Basically."

Elisabeth frowned. "Can I have her number? Maybe I can call her to at least have some idea what she would like?"

Byron shook his head. "It wouldn't do you much good. I tell you what. You're a woman. You have womanly preferences. Why don't you choose a couple of colors, and we can go with that?"

Elisabeth looked even more confused than before. He was doing the best he could. This would only be hard if she made it so.

"Think of it as a blank canvas," he said.

She nodded slowly and turned to her iPad to type. Before she could finish, Byron heard a commotion outside his study door.

He looked up in time to see his sister bursting in.

"I'm family," Angie said to Lana, who trailed behind her.

Lana looked at Byron with a worried expression. He held his hand up to reassure her. "It's OK."

Lana reluctantly turned and left the room. Angie continued to march toward the table, unbothered by the commotion she caused.

"I need to talk to you," Angie said without acknowledgement of Elisabeth.

The planner's response was to gather her iPad and briefcase to leave.

"I'm sorry for the interruption. When would be a good time to follow up with you?" Byron said.

"Uh, I'll call you in a week to let you know what I've come up with," Elisabeth responded.

"Mmm, we better make it two days. We're on a tight schedule. Gotta keep the wheels on this bus moving."

She nodded and rushed out the door. He would have felt sorry for her, but this was her job. He was paying her top dollar to deliver a quality wedding on time, on budget. She could do it. He wouldn't have hired her if she couldn't.

"What bus?" Angie asked as Elisabeth was closing the door.

"Oh, this wedding."

Angie's eyes grew as big as saucers. "Who's getting married?"

"Erica."

"Really? To who?"

"This young man she met a couple of months ago."

"Wow. That's fast."

"No need to waste time."

"Is she ready?" Angie sat in the spot Elisabeth had left.

"She'd better be," Byron said, thinking about the impending baby. He didn't think this was the right time to tell Angie about it.

"Oh, I don't know. A lot of bad can happen if she's not."

"Maybe the stability will be good for her. She can't keep running rampant forever. Acting like the world is one big party. It's time for her to get serious about life and lay down some roots."

Angie shook her head. "If you say so, brother."

"I know so."

She scanned the table. "Where is my invite?"

Byron hesitated. He wasn't sure what to say. Erica hadn't been warm to Angie in years. It had gotten worse since she took the baby for her. She wouldn't like the idea of Angie coming to the wedding. "We haven't created them yet."

"You have my address."

"Yeeeeah." He drew the word out.

She raised an eyebrow. "What?"

He sighed. "Do you think it's a good idea?"

"For what?"

"For you to come to the wedding?"

"Why would I not come? It's my niece, isn't it?"

Byron could hear the hurt in his sister's voice. He wasn't trying to make her feel bad. Under the circumstances, he thought she might want to lay low.

"Right, but given everything … I was thinking it might not be a good idea. I mean, how do you think she's going to feel?"

"I don't know. She doesn't talk to me."

"That's my point."

"I've tried reaching out to her. It's like I did something wrong. I even offered to let her see the child. She rebuffed that so quickly."

"She's not interested in it. I could have told you that," Byron said. Quite frankly, neither was he.

"Either way, I don't know what I've done to her other than help handle this, this situation and, speaking of such, that's why I'm here."

Byron looked at his sister. She made a money motion with her hand.

"Not this again. I've given you money. What do you need it for now?" he asked.

"This girl has more doctors' bills than I can keep up with."

"Babies have doctors' visits."

"I know that. I raised a son. He didn't have as many issues as her. I need some help."

Byron sighed. Why didn't he give the child up? "C'mon, Angie. We gotta reel this in."

"I think they're getting closer with the treatment."

"They'd better. The money train is about to stop." Byron's phone vibrated on the table. He picked it up and saw a text. It was from Patrick, the investigator. *I'm ready. Tell me when*, the text said. Patrick had the information. It was time to get the low down on his wife and Alonzo.

"They will. I'm so grateful I can depend on you to come through for me. We always got each other. You got me and I got you," Angie said.

Byron was barely able to pull himself away from the text to hear his sister's rambling. He had asked her to help cover up many things in the past. He was always getting in a mess and she was always swooping in to clean it up. He needed his sister to stay in his corner, as always. Who knew what he'd find out when he met with Patrick. He texted a time and place to meet, while his sister continued babbling on.

Chapter 31

The Real

yron decided to meet Patrick at a restaurant this time. The Open Table was a popular spot that had garnered a lot of press. He chose it because they had an exclusive VIP room in the back that most people didn't know about. If they entered through a back door, no one would see them meeting there. Byron wiggled around in his seat as he waited for the hostess to usher his visitor to the back. He found himself looking at the clock. What did Patrick find? When the investigator called, Byron should have asked for a hint. He thought about all the things he might find out and decided that he should stop thinking about it, even though he was getting more worked up by the second. His phone finally buzzed and he saw the text from Patrick. *I'm here*, it said.

Byron turned toward the door and spotted him walking his way. Patrick sat across from him and nodded before placing a large brown envelope on the table in front of him. Byron eyed it, as if he would be able to see through it and read the contents.

"A lot warmer outside today," Patrick said with a slight smile, seemingly oblivious to Byron's suppressed urgency.

Byron nodded in politeness.

"Should we order?" Patrick asked.

Byron wanted to shout "No" but figured there was no reason to be rude. He would get the information he needed, even if he had to threaten it out of him. "Sure."

They ordered. Unwilling to wait any longer, Byron jumped in as soon as the waitress left. "So are you ready to get started?'

"Of course," Patrick cleared his throat. "I know you must be eager to find out what I came up with. Before I reveal it, I want you to know that people usually aren't prepared for what they get."

Byron frowned. "I think I can handle it."

"I've had situations where a client was expecting their suspicious to be unfounded and get surprised when it's worse than they thought. They were totally disappointed and sometimes blamed me for it."

"Ridiculous. You won't have to worry about that." Patrick's warning worried him, but he retold himself that he could handle whatever was disclosed. The question was would he be able to control his temper.

Patrick opened the envelope. "The first thing I did was follow your wife. As you know, she doesn't go too many places, unless they are for enjoyment. I did spot her in a couple of visits to a fertility doctor's office."

Patrick dropped a photo of her coming out of the office with shades on.

Byron scanned it. "Yeah, she's been trying to get me to have a baby. I'm not sure about that yet."

"Well, it looks like she's still set on it. I saw her leaving the office with another man in tow. At first, I thought he might be the husband of a patient she ran into. This photo convinced me otherwise."

Patrick showed Byron a picture of Veronica hugging and kissing their gardener. There it was a visual of something he already knew, except it looked like she got tired of waiting for him to give her the baby and went on her own to make it happen.

On one hand, he wasn't surprised. Veronica was the type that expected to always live the good life. It stood to reason she'd do whatever she could to get it, yet this seemed low, even for her. Using the gardener to have a baby. He supposed she thought he'd be too stupid to see that the baby was Mexican and willingly fork over thousands per month in child support. One thing was for sure: he would make her pay for trying to play him. And it would cost her dearly.

"I'm sorry," Patrick said.

Byron shook his head. "You found what I needed. What else?"

"Well, you wanted me to watch Alonzo and, of course, I did."

"And?" Byron asked, coming out of his vengeful trance to get more details.

Patrick pulled a picture out. "I found him coming out of an unknown house." He showed Byron a picture, in which Alonzo was getting into his car.

"This is the woman." Patrick showed another picture with her and Alonzo in a tight embrace. Byron squinted, trying to recognize the woman. He didn't. She was nothing special. Long, brown hair. Big breasts.

"I take it that's not your daughter."

Byron looked up from the picture and leaned back, rubbing his chin.

"There's more."

"Women?" Byron asked.

"No. Well, yeah. However, I don't think this was a date. Alonzo had another meeting that I didn't expect. Do you know these people?" He pushed the picture across the table.

It showed Alonzo standing around talking to Angie and Leon.

Byron snatched the photo.

Patrick jumped back but kept talking.

"I was really confused. Does Alonzo know this other guy?"

"I don't think so." What the hell was going on here? Did Alonzo meet Leon at his annual party and Byron just didn't remember it? Perhaps Erica introduced the two. Even that seemed like a really strange possibility, especially if there was any flirting going on. He shuddered at the thought. And how did Angie end up all chummy with those two? As far as he knew, she had never even met Alonzo. She even acted like she didn't know about his engagement to Erica.

There was something fishy going on. Byron could tell that something wasn't right if for no other reason than that all of this was happening behind his back. Alliances were forming without his knowledge or participation. He smelled a mutiny rising. He would be cutting straight through any plans they were forming against him or Erica.

Patrick hadn't said anything. He was staring at Byron like a spectator watches a bear at the zoo. After sitting with the information he had, Byron finally sighed and said, "Thank you for all of your work. This gives me a lot to think about. Would you be able to continue this research?"

Patrick's eyebrows almost shot up to his hair line. "Really?"

"Yeah, your perspective has been useful. I want to continue finding out what's going on. I will double your fee."

Patrick smiled hard. "Thank you. Sure. What else do you need?"

"I want you to follow someone else too."

***

Byron sat at the head of his dining room table, carefully eating casserole, tilapia and tender baby carrots. Right as he was about to put another bite of fish in his mouth, Veronica ran into the room like a hurricane. She *looked* like a storm too. Her hair was wild and in the wind. Her face was flushed. He could tell she was flustered.

"What do you think you're doing?" Veronica said, standing to the side of him. She placed her hand firmly on her hip for emphasis. Something that didn't impress upon Byron to answer her any faster.

He took his time chewing the fish and swallowing before he washed it down with a swig of Chardonnay. "I'm eating. What's the problem?"

"You did something to my credit card."

Byron shot her his best innocent look. He didn't know how good he was at it. She didn't look convinced. "It still works, right?"

"No, the store told me that I had reached my limit. You have some explaining to do."

He put his hand over his chest. "Pardon me?"

"Don't play dumb. You always have money and this hasn't happened before. You did this to me."

"I didn't do anything to you. I simply had to make some changes to some accounts. It involved lowering some of the limits."

"But you pay the bills. There's no reason for that to happen unless you initiated it. Are you still angry with me about Erica?"

Byron sighed. "No. Look. Even though Erica's wedding will be relatively small, it's still going to cost a pretty penny, especially since she wants other people to do all the work. This is to make sure we don't go in the hole trying to take care of her."

"What does that have to do with the card?"

Veronica refused to come off that card. Inside, Byron was loving it. She was sweating because she couldn't go ball out like she wanted. Well, that was too bad. Maybe she should get used to it because when they go their separate ways, that's exactly what she was going to experience, especially with a man like Jose.

"It's money. Do you know that Erica got a card in my name and ran it up? I owe that now."

"So . . . make her pay it back."

"She doesn't have any money to pay it back."

"And you're putting a wedding on for her?"

"It's in the backyard. Besides, she's still my daughter."

"Who cares? We'd have another child, if you didn't dawdle. I'm telling you I'm not going to wait forever," Veronica threatened.

"What are you going to do? Divorce me?" Byron asked.

It became so quiet in the dining room that they could hear a pin drop. The two stared at each other. Byron swore he could see Veronica flinch a little. She wasn't as tough as she liked to make it seem. *Go ahead and say you want a divorce. So you can leave here with nothing.* In his head, Byron dared her to say she wanted to leave with that broke gardener. He could find another Veronica. She would have a hard time finding another Byron. She finally gave up the staring contest and left the room, which is what she should have done.

Chapter 32

Pre-Wedding Worries

Erica sauntered into the bathroom right as Alonzo was coming out of the shower. He hadn't said much to her since the baby party. Her woman's intuition told her the argument between her and Veronica bothered him. He was so upset when he heard about her first child. She was certain that Cruella's accusations rubbed him the wrong way all over again. He probably didn't believe her when she denied everything that Veronica said, but over time he should come around. He had to— they had a new baby on the way. No time to be petty. Yet he was a bit chilly to her.

Alonzo was standing in the middle of the bathroom, naked and wet. She ran her hand down his back as he reached on the rack for a towel.

"What do you have scheduled for today?" she asked.

"A few meetings," He ran the towel over his face and down his arms.

She reached for the towel to dry his back. He pulled it back.

"I got it," he said.

Definitely still angry. She had some work to do. "I'm going shopping today. Is there anything I can get for you?"

"Uh. No. Well, wait. I do have to meet with a potential client tomorrow. I'm trying to convince her to work with me for her first attempt at the music industry. I wanna get her something to show that she's with a winner." He turned and faced her, his nakedness on full display. "Do you think you can handle that?"

Erica felt a sharp pang of jealousy, which she'd never had in her relationship with Alonzo. It wasn't enough for her to acknowledge out loud. It was enough for her to take notice. She swallowed it and kept talking. "Sure. Under one condition."

He frowned. "What?"

She held her finger to his lips while moving closer to him. She ran her hands down his chest and kneeled. Erica moved her hands down to his shaft, picking up his flaccid member. She flicked her tongue around it. By the time she pushed it into her mouth, his erection indicated that he was fully on board with her condition. He leaned back against the wall, completely giving in to her. She felt so powerful and in control, but she hadn't missed the implications. Something was wrong. She hoped it wasn't too serious.

In the meantime, Erica figured she would try to make it right by doing as promised. She went shopping and picked up a bracelet for $250 at a cute high end shop. That should impress some little girl trying to come up in the world. The feeling she had earlier that morning started to nag her again. Everything was set. They were getting married the day after tomorrow in a no muss, no fuss ceremony. She was preparing for the baby on the way. She hadn't even been having any morning sickness. They should be happy, but Alonzo was getting more and more cranky. She forced herself to push it out of her mind, continuing to shop for herself and the baby. She was also on the lookout for things that would cheer Alonzo up.

After a shopping spree, lunch and an afternoon movie, Erica finally found her way home, confident that the rest of the day would be better. Her interactions with Alonzo would be improved, especially since she bought an awesome gift. However, she discovered that she was wrong the minute she walked through the door.

"Where were you earlier today?" Alonzo barked.

Erica stumbled backward. "I was out running some errands."

"I called you several times. You didn't answer."

"I'm sorry. My phone was off for a while. The battery was running low. So I was trying to save the juice." She dropped her bags and reached for her phone. Erica turned it on, immediately seeing all his missed calls and texts.

Alonzo walked closer to her. "If you can't keep your phone charged while you're outside the house, perhaps you should stay home until I get here."

"What?"

"That way you always have access to a phone."

"I said I was sorry. There's no need to get extreme," Erica said. He was totally overreacting.

"Then keep your phone on and charged. As a matter of fact, I want you to sign out and in every time you leave the house."

There was no way he would make her sign out to leave the house. "You've gotta be out of your fucking mind."

"That way I always know where you are."

"I'm not signing anything. I'm gonna be your wife. Not your employee."

"I need you to be in place."

"I'll be where I am. Now when you come up with a better idea to stay connected, you let me know." Erica picked up her bags to leave the room.

Alonzo grabbed a couple of them from her.

"Hey. Give me that back!"

He reached into the bag, pulled out the clothes and tore them apart.

Erica screamed. "What the hell are you doing? I just bought that." She struggled with him for control of the bags and the clothes until he pushed her backward. She fell to the floor, hitting her head on a nearby chair. "Ouch." She rubbed the back of her head.

He panted and stared at her. "Now they're junk." He walked out of the room.

She couldn't believe what happened. How could he do that to her? She cried right there on the floor.

After a few minutes, she got up from the floor, leaving her bags and the torn clothes there. Erica went into the bathroom and took a shower, wiping away a few more tears under the water beating down on her skin. She finally got dressed in a satin night gown and crawled into bed. She bypassed dinner, preferring to sleep her hurt and frustration away. She thought Alonzo would leave her be. She wasn't so lucky.

The bedroom door opened and he entered carrying a tray.

"Hey," he said.

She tensed and ignored him. He rounded to her side of the bed with the tray. She looked over her shoulder at the plate of food and side of grape juice. He sat it on the bed. Clearly, he wasn't going to leave her alone. She sat up a little.

"Alright, sleeping beauty. Here's your dinner."

"I'm not hungry," Erica mumbled.

"You need to eat something."

"Not if I'm not hungry."

"You have to eat something for the baby." He gave her a cloth napkin. He looked at her cheery and expectant. She didn't feel the same. So she grabbed the napkin quickly from his grasp.

"How have you been sleeping?" he asked

"Fine."

He sat to watch her. She slowly pressed her fork into some veggies and stopped when she felt him looking at her. "What are you looking at?"

"My wife."

Erica sucked her teeth. "I don't wanna hear that bullshit."

He leaned over to kiss her lips. She moved away. He sat back and sighed.

"I'm sorry for my behavior today. I was out of line."

Erica continued to play with her food.

"Please accept my apology." He ran his hand over hers. "I got upset when I couldn't reach you. I didn't know what happened. You're carrying my baby."

"That's no excuse."

"I know. Don't give up on us. It won't happen again. I promise that. I'm gonna replace all the clothes I destroyed."

She wanted to believe that things would get better, but she had a hard time seeing that. He wasn't going to change. So she would have to deal with it. Who else would take care of her and the baby? What else would she do? Move back home with her father? She couldn't deal with Veronica again. She really would have to kill her.

"OK," Erica said, allowing doubt to seep into her voice.

"Great. I'll take you on a big shopping spree after our wedding," he smiled, "Are you ready?"

"Always ready to shop."

Alonzo chuckled. "No, are you ready to be Mrs. Slade?"

No, but what other choice did she have. Everything was set. Nothing left to do but put her big girl draws on and move forward. Erica grabbed the juice off the tray and turned it up to her lips after saying, "Can't wait."

Chapter 33

It's Almost Time

The big day had arrived. Alonzo and Erica were to wed in Byron's backyard. It was tight, but the wedding planner pulled it off. Elisabeth had arranged a platform with eight vases filled with white flowers. Additional vases and candles lined the area Erica would walk. It was beautiful.

Elisabeth also ordered the photographer, Aiden, to come early so they could set up and start taking photos. Erica posed near a tree in the backyard, a little way from the house and the set-up for her wedding. Her hair blew softly in the wind. Byron looked up at the slight overcast but pushed his concerns back down. It wasn't supposed to rain.

"Perfect. Your make-up is exquisite," Aiden said, in his Australian accent.

"Thank you. It's my best work," Byron chimed.

The photographer chuckled, while Erica seemed less amused. Byron wondered if she knew about Alonzo's escapades. He searched his daughter's face for sadness, anger, something. She was like a statue.

"Alright, Erica. It's on the portal you can go and post it," Aiden said.

"Post?" Byron asked.

"In case I want to post it on social media." Erica moved away from the tree.

They both started to walk back to the house. "Oh. Is everything else set?" he asked.

"I hope so. I'm glad this is small. It's already too much work."

Byron nodded. "So you haven't changed your mind?"

Erica frowned. "About what?"

"The wedding."

Erica stopped walking. "Why would I do that?"

Byron paused. "Because you look like something's bothering you. I'd understand if you have doubts. You barely know him." It hadn't even been a full two months. Before, Byron was more concerned about her getting out of the house by his deadline. Now he was more concerned about the man she was marrying. This whole plan was shaping up to be a bad idea.

"I know him well enough to be pregnant from him." Her voice elevated toward the end.

Byron scanned the yard and moved closer to her. "You don't need to let the whole world know that."

"Why not? They'll find out soon anyway." Erica's lip quivered slightly.

"Our relationship has been strained over the last several years, but I'm still your father. You don't have to do anything you don't want to do. I'll support you." He stared deep into his daughter's eyes, trying to relay his intent on looking out for her. He still couldn't tell if she knew about the other women. If she were this upset, she had to know, right?

Erica took a deep breath. "I appreciate that but," she looked at the perfectly manicured grass. "maybe you've been right all along. It's time for me to grow up and take responsibility for my actions. I've ran wild long enough."

She didn't look convinced to him. She appeared to be trying to make sense of her decision to wed this man, a man Byron knew she didn't love. For a brief minute, he felt responsible. Perhaps this wouldn't have happened if he'd taken a different approach with her.

She reached over and hugged her father. "I gotta finish getting ready."

Byron nodded and watched her walk off. He felt compelled to fix this or at the very least lessen the damage. Erica and Alonzo would not live happily ever after. He went into the house looking for his soon-to-be son-in-law.

As caterers and decorators hustled and bustled around the house, Byron caught a glimpse of

Alonzo standing in the middle of the floor, looking lost. He turned to and fro as if he were trying hard to figure out what was going on. He seemed nervous.

"Are you alright?" Byron approached him.

"Huh? Yeah. Sure," Alonzo said.

Byron put his arm around Alonzo's shoulder. "Come this way."

They entered the pool room. Byron gave him a stick. "Let's take a few shots. It might help you relax."

Lana found them and came into the room with a couple of drinks. The two men grabbed them. As she walked out the door, Byron watched Alonzo down his drink in one big swig.

He raised an eyebrow. "Better."

Alonzo sighed and nodded.

They quietly started a game. Byron gave him a minute or two before leaning into him. "Are you ready to be a husband?"

Alonzo struck the ball with his pool stick. "As ready as I'll ever be."

"What do you mean?"

"I've reached that time in my life where a family is the next step. Erica and I will do well."

"You know, being the head of household isn't as easy as it looks."

"I don't expect it to be easy, but I believe that we'll make it."

This from a man that had been photographed with another woman days before his wedding. Byron may have chuckled if the woman he cheated on wasn't his own daughter. Alonzo's cavalier attitude only made him angry. It was time to move in for the kill.

"I wanted to talk to you about your future." Byron positioned his stick.

"Oh?"

Byron shot the ball across the table. "For a while now, I've been reviewing music for artists all over the world. Some are horrible. Some have real talent. The problem is they need some development. Do you still want to work in the music industry?"

Alonzo raised an eyebrow. "Absolutely."

Byron nodded. "I'm excited to hear that. I want to extend an offer for you to work for me under my new management company."

Alonzo's mouth dropped open. Byron smiled slightly.

"Really? Wow. That would be great."

Byron could tell he didn't expect the offer. Alonzo looked perplexed, like he wasn't sure what else to say. There's no way he could turn this down without appearing suspect.

"What are the details?" Alonzo asked.

"I'm glad you asked. You can work from home. I'll set it up for you to get the music. You'll contact the artists, arrange meetings, check them out, see if they are worth developing. You'll be responsible for crafting their image, sound, etc."

"How will we make money?"

Byron smiled. "I'll start you off with 95k a year and a commission for the ones that make money. And because you are marrying my daughter, I'm going to buy you all a house. As a matter of fact," Byron walked to a nearby drawer and pulled out a picture of a house, "I'll close on this beauty by the end of the week."

Alonzo stared at the large home on the picture with six bedrooms, six baths, a game room, summer kitchen and an Olympic-sized pool. "Aww, man. That's beautiful."

"Is that a yes?"

"Absolutely. I even have some artists lined up. I was going to ask you about them. They're gonna explode soon."

"Excellent. Like a man that's ahead of the game." Under the picture of the house, Byron pulled out a small stack of papers. Alonzo's face went from a smile to a frown. Byron moved along as if he didn't see it. "This is the contract. If you want to take a few minutes to look over it, you can."

Alonzo grabbed it slowly and leafed through it. "Uh, what does it say?"

"It outlines the conditions of your employment. It's a good agreement. You can sign now." Byron extended a pen to him.

Alonzo read the contract closer, squinting as his eyes focused on certain parts. "What's section four about?"

"That's saying if we should part ways for any reason, assets accumulated as a result of this agreement will remain with the company."

"Assets?"

"Yes. It's really standard."

"Is that including my personal assets?"

Byron nodded. "It can." The truth was he made it so that Alonzo would never be able to do anything to him or Erica without suffering some legal or personal retribution. Byron watched him struggle with whether he should sign or not. He took a drink.

"Um, I'm gonna have to think on this," Alonzo finally said.

"That's understandable. I wouldn't think too long. The offer is good for twenty-four hours. After that, it could change."

Alonzo glanced at the contract again. Byron stifled his amusement. The young man had no idea what to do, but it was only a matter of time until he signed the paper. Since Byron put a deadline on it. He likely would do it today. There was no way he would go to sleep tonight with that contract on his head, especially when he was being offered more than he could give Erica on his own. Byron was doing him a favor, even though it came at more of a benefit to Byron. If there was one thing he'd learned in the entertainment industry over the years, it was that enemies really did need to be close, especially when they were connected to the family. This way, when he went in for a fatherly hug, Alonzo wouldn't always see the knife going into his back.

Chapter 34

Can't Believe It

Fresh off his man-to-man with Alonzo, Byron went back up front in time to hear the doorbell ring. He started to ignore it, but it kept ringing and no one was moving to answer it.

Still your house, Byron thought.

He opened the door. To his unpleasant surprise, he saw his sister, Angie. Byron thought he told her it wasn't a good idea for her to be there. He had planned to talk to her later and warn her that if she did anything fishy he would cut her off and report her as an unfit guardian. As he gave her a once over at the door, he would probably make a good case. Angie looked flustered and slightly disheveled.

"What are you doing here?"

"I have to talk to you," she said gruffly as she shuffled into the house.

He closed the door behind her.

"Is there somewhere we can talk privately?"

"Yeah." Byron took her into the guesthouse. He would have gone into his study, but he knew his sister well enough to know whatever she was about to say wouldn't be good. They needed to be farther away from everybody. Once they were in the house and far from guests' earshot, he closed the door behind him. "What is it?"

Angie rubbed her hands together nervously. She shook all over.

"Talk. What's going on?" Byron asked, trying to mask the worry in his voice.

"How could you make me take that child?"

He scowled. "You asked, and I pay you to do it."

"You're going to have to pay me more."

The picture of her with Leon and Alonzo immediately popped into his head. He felt like a shakedown was coming and here it was. "Why?"

Angie pointed at him. "You know why. Sneaky snake."

"What the hell are you talking about?"

"Don't act stupid. I raised you better than that." At this point, she had tears in her eyes. She pushed Byron.

He regained his balance. "What's your problem?"

"You're gonna pay me for this." She grabbed his shirt and shook him.

"Let go of me. You're not making any sense. What's wrong with you?"

"Your daughter . . . your daughter," she said between gasps.

"What?"

"She seduced my son."

This time it was Byron's turn to push. "What the fuck are you talking about?"

"She spread her legs to my son and had that baby. You knew, and you didn't even tell me. How dare you?"

"That's the stupidest thing you've ever said. Where did you get that shit from?"

Angie covered her face and tried to collect herself. "I told you the baby has problems."

"So? I gave you money to pay for the hospital bills."

"The doctors kept taking more and more blood tests. Trying to figure out why she was sick all the time and," she sobbed, "they found out that the baby has parents that are related."

Byron turned away quickly. "No, no. That's some kind of mistake. The doctor is wrong."

"He's right. They've figured it out, and I want more money for this or I'm going to talk."

He turned back to her and grabbed her arm and squeezed. "What did you say? You'd better watch it."

"Ow." She snatched her arm away. "You watch it. I want $3,000 more a month. No exceptions."

"I don't do threats. Why would you do this to me?"

"You know what I know. So if you know what's best for you, give me what I ask for." Angie stormed off.

"Angie! Come back here."

She slammed the door behind her. He opened it and followed her, his heart beating fast. Byron, unsuccessfully, tried to calm himself. He was shaking like his sister. Angie ran down the hill, passing guests starting to arrive.

He couldn't believe it. There had to be some kind of mistake. Involving the courts would be a nightmare. Everyone would know about her accusations. At the same time, $3,000 more per month was far too much money to pay her to keep quiet. Then again, what if this was a set up? Some plan she concocted with Leon and Alonzo. There was no way his daughter would do something so immoral as to sleep with her own cousin. Forget the wedding—he needed to talk to her now.

He dashed into the house and up the stairs, asking every few people if they saw Erica. Byron finally located her in the bathroom in one of the rooms down the hall. She was perched up on a high chair getting her make-up done.

"Daddy, what are you doing in here? I'm not ready yet," she said.

Byron motioned to the makeup artist. "I need to talk to my daughter alone, please."

"Can't this wait? We start in forty-five minutes," Erica said.

"No, it can't."

"But we don't have time."

"We have to talk now," he demanded.

Erica and the make-up artist jumped. She stared at him, while the artist hurried out of the bathroom. He closed the door behind her, leaning on the doorknob for support. Byron needed it from somewhere after what he was about to ask Erica.

"Your aunt was here."

"What? Did you invite her? I want her gone," Erica shouted.

"No, I didn't invite her, and she's already gone."

"Are you sure? I don't wanna see her, Daddy."

There was the entry he needed. Byron took a deep breath and turned to face her. "Why don't you want to see her?"

She rolled her eyes. "You know why. I don't need any drama," Erica looked in the mirror to push a lock of hair away from her freshly applied foundation. "We don't need it."

"What is it you're not telling me?" Byron asked.

"Nothing. I just want this day to go as smoothly as possible," Erica said, still fixed on her reflection.

Byron narrowed his eyes. "Don't lie to me, girl."

She stopped manipulating her hair and slowly faced her father. Byron edged closer to her. His eyes bore into her like laser beams, daring her to act nonchalant at a time like this.

Her eyes got bigger, frightened looking. "What are you talking about?"

"I'm gonna ask you a question. You'd better think long and hard about how you want to answer. I don't want any lies. I need the truth. Do you understand?"

Erica nodded.

"Who's the father of that baby?"

Chapter 35

Moment of Truth

Erica couldn't remember the last time she saw her father so upset. She tried to imagine what her trifling aunt had said, but she couldn't. This was the wrong day to think of such craziness.

"Alonzo," she answered, hoping that was the answer her father was looking for. She could tell by the vein coming out of his neck that it wasn't.

"Not that one," he shouted. He inhaled and exhaled slowly. "Who is the father of the other one?"

"Oh, Daddy. This is not the time to discuss this."

"Erica? You better answer me." His voice was low, yet there was nothing soft or comforting about it. The sound was like the calm before an unruly storm.

"Why?"

"Because I said so."

"That's ridiculous. This is unnecessary." She couldn't believe he was asking her this.

"Erica . . ."

"Really? What is this about?" Her voice raised a few more decibels and quivered at the end.

"You've let this go on long enough. You need to tell me the truth." Now, he looked worried.

Tears welled in her eyes. "Why would you make me?"

"Because it's serious!" He shouted.

She had a sinking feeling in her stomach. "What are you talking about?"

He grabbed her arm. "Answer my question. Who impregnated you?"

"I can't." Her bottom lip quivered, as she barely got the words out between sobs.

"You can't what?"

"I can't say it." She wasn't feeling so good.

Byron leaned forward until he was eye to eye with Erica. "Why didn't you tell me?"

Erica covered her mouth and dove for the toilet. She held on to it while her stomach retched. She heard how horrible she sounded and it was hard to care. She just wanted to get it over with. After a couple of minutes of turning her insides out, she staggered to the sink. While she splashed water around in her mouth, she could hear her father walking closer to her.

"Why did you let me find out this way? Do you know how much trouble we're in?"

For the first time ever, Erica heard her father's voice crack. It broke her heart a little more. She couldn't remember the last time she heard her father cry. She was certain she never had. Shame and guilt wore on her like a bag of bricks.

"How did it happen?" he asked.

Erica sobbed. "Please."

"Did he throw himself on you? Or did you seduce him?"

She faced her father. "No! How could you even think I'd do that? I handled it all by myself! No one helped me through this. I did the best I could."

"You shut down and didn't say a word."

"What was I supposed to say?" Erica swallowed the wave of nausea threatening to reappear. "That he abused and raped me? No one would have understood what I was going through. Would you have believed me? Or Aunt Angie? Maybe you would've blamed me."

"If you had told me the truth, I would've helped you."

"Then help me now!"

Her father seemed to scrutinize her. She couldn't tell what he was thinking. Would he kick her out of the house again? He finally nodded.

"OK. OK." He pulled her to him and hugged her. The hug was slightly snug at first. Then, it got tighter as the seconds went by. Erica told herself she didn't need it. However, the cry that escaped her throat said differently. Her father held on to her while she released years of anger, hurt, and shame. Her secret was finally out, as excruciating as it was. Now what? How would she move on?

She had another baby growing inside of her. Perhaps making her or his life better was a start. This may be a good time to see what her father thought. "What are we going to do?"

"We're going to gather evidence," he said.

Erica looked at her father. "Are you talking about pressing charges?"

"Yes. For assault and extortion."

She frowned. "What? Am I missing something?"

He sighed. "Angie is asking for more money or she'll make this public."

"What?" Erica shouted. "I can't—"

Her father placed his hands over her arms. "Don't worry. I'm handling that. Among other things and because of those things." He paused. "You shouldn't marry Alonzo."

Her eyes grew wide. "Are you kidding? There are 100 people outside waiting."

"He's in it with Angie."

"No, he doesn't know Aunt Angie."

Her father pulled out his phone and pressed his finger on Pictures. Up popped photos of Alonzo hugged up with another woman. Her heart sunk. The nerve of him to do this to her while she was pregnant with his baby. Her father swiped left, and photos of Alonzo talking to her aunt and Leon appeared. *What the . . . !* How did Alonzo know her aunt? And Leon? The bastard was trying to ruin her family. All for money. She was now angry and scared but not sure she should tell her father about her connection to Leon.

"What is this?"

"That's what I've been finding out. Angie's threat today must have something to do with it," her father said.

"This is a nightmare." Erica put her head in her hands.

"Listen to me." Her father shook her arms. "You have to hold it together.

She sniffed. "So what do you want me to do?"

Chapter 36

Bones

Byron left Erica upstairs. She was still barely consolable. He decided it was best that he make the announcement that the wedding was off. As he went back downstairs, he wondered if it was a good idea to get Erica some therapy. This was a heavy situation. She had to need help dealing with it. He certainly wasn't the right person to get her through it.

He stared out the window at the backyard now filled with guests, many he didn't even know very well. His spirit felt heavy. It was the weight of his facade, act of having it all together. He began running over what he would tell them when a young man approaching the house caught his attention. He wore a black tuxedo. So he was dressed for the wedding, yet he didn't quite look like he belonged.

Byron went to open the door to see him clearly and felt his pulse quicken when he recognized him. It was Leon.

Byron stepped outside and closed the door behind him. He stood on the front steps with his arms crossed. Leon approached sheepishly.

"What the hell are you doing here?" Byron barked at Leon.

"Sorry to bother you, sir. I was wondering if Erica is here."

"Why do you want to know?"

Leon raised an eyebrow. He stretched his neck to see inside. "It looks like there's a wedding going on."

"There is." Byron crossed his arms.

Leon smirked. "I heard that she was getting married, and I wanted to wish her well and maybe stay to cheer when she says 'I do.'"

"That won't be necessary. I'll let her know you stopped by." Byron turned to leave. Leon stepped forward.

"I wouldn't do that. You see, I have some information about you and your family and if you don't let me in and do what I say, I'll make sure everyone on this property knows about it."

Byron wanted to smash his face in right there, but before he could raise his hand, Leon opened his jacket to reveal a Beretta. He recognized the gun because he'd possessed a few around the house. Unfortunately, they weren't nearby. On the other hand, he did have a gun in the study. Perfect place to lead Leon.

"C'mon." Byron opened the door. Leon followed him down the hall, passed trays of hors d'oeuvres and alcoholic beverages. The men moved smoothly as if nothing were wrong and almost made it to the study door when Veronica stopped them.

"There you are. The yard is filling up fast." She glanced over his shoulder and saw Leon. Her eyes moved back and forth between the two men. "Hello."

Leon nodded.

"Something's come up. There's going to be a delay," Byron said.

"A delay? For how long? We have all these people here," she said.

"I'll talk to you in a minute." Byron moved around her with Leon in tow.

As soon as they entered the study, Leon locked the door. Byron walked behind his desk, making sure he was within arm's reach of his gun.

"What do you want?" Byron asked.

Leon smiled. "Now you're concerned about what I want?"

"I don't have time for the games. In case you hadn't noticed, guests are outside waiting for a wedding. I need to address them."

"Figures. You've always been too selfish to think about anybody but yourself. I used to look up to you."

I don't care. That's what Byron wanted to say, but he hadn't forgotten about the gun on Leon's side. Byron shrugged.

"Oh, so you don't care, huh?"

"What are you trying to do? It's time for you to man up and explain what this is all about."

"You know what this is about."

"No, I don't."

Leon pulled out his gun. "See, playing me for a fool is not a good idea."

"So what? You gonna shoot me?" Byron put his hand on the desk, closer to his hidden gun.

"If you make me." Leon inhaled and exhaled. "Stick to the plan," the young man mumbled to himself before turning his attention back to Byron. "You're gonna transfer 10 million into my account or I'm gonna tell everybody here what kind of disgusting family you have."

Byron felt his skin almost burst into flames. There was no way he would pay this boy anything to keep any secret. "You can insult my family all you want, but deep down you want to be a part of it, and it bothers you that you're not. Get over it."

Leon leaped around the desk and leaned on Byron, pointing his gun at him. "You know who my family is. You were too chicken to step up and be a man. Take responsibility for your actions. You have to pay now. One way or the other.”

Byron looked beyond the barrel in his face and into the eyes of the young man. They were lonely, angry eyes. He seemed to resent the world but more specifically Byron. “No one can make you feel better about the past. You’re gonna have to move on.”

“Shut up! Don’t you tell me what to do. It’s a little late for that.” Leon scowled and waved his gun around. “All your career you’ve moved along like you don’t have a care in the world. That stops today.”

Byron was sure Leon didn’t really want to kill him—he just wanted to see him humiliated in front of everybody. A pang of guilt pierced through him. He never wanted Leon, and now he was facing the fallout.

“Is that why you’ve been reaching out to my sister and Erica’s husband? To make things hard for me?”

Leon chuckled but without any real amusement. "That was to get money from you. I was surprised by how gullible you were. You actually gave your sister all that money. I have to admit it was big of you to mention me to your sister. She was happy to see me. Her long-lost nephew. Didn't even hold back on telling me about all the things you were doing for the baby. I guess you do care about the little girl, huh?"

Byron should have gotten an investigator much sooner. He knew something wasn't right, but he was too busy dealing with his trifling wife and troubled daughter that he didn't want to go the extra step to figure out what was going on. And he'd paid for it. He would not pay for it anymore.

"I'm not giving you any more money."

"Do you know what I will do to you?"

Byron responded in a calm tone. "I don't care. No matter how much you try to hurt me it will not ease the anger and the hurt you have from my absence in your life. You gotta let that go."

"I told you! Don't tell me what to do."

Someone knocked on the study door. When Leon glanced at the door, Byron took the opportunity to shove Leon, causing him to almost topple over. Before Byron could reach for the gun in his desk, Leon recovered and started to point his gun toward him. The two men struggled with the gun. It fired, hitting a light fixture. There were more knocks on the door, accompanied with banging—in obvious response to the gunfire. Byron and Leon still struggled with the gun. Byron heard the sound of a tool, like a hatchet, coming down on the door. He started slamming Leon up against the desk. He finally head butted him. When he staggered backward, Byron tried to loosen the gun from his grip, but he was still holding on for dear life. Byron was able to point the gun away from him toward the wall and made one last attempt to make him lose his grip.

At that moment, the door opened. A few people rushed in, and the gun fired. Stunned, Byron and Leon froze. A bloody circle formed on a white shirt.

Epilogue, One Year Later

It seemed like yesterday when things really started to fall apart for Erica. Her life had been hard enough, but having her worst secret come out felt like it would kill her. Luckily, it didn't, and while some things had fallen apart, such as Jose catching the bullet from Leon's gun and dying, there had been some improvements.

Leon was finally imprisoned for extortion and manslaughter for Jose's death. Aunt Angie was also charged in the money scheme, but she was given probation, which allowed her to continue to raise Megan. Erica had a healthy baby boy, who she named Byron after her father. Perhaps most importantly, she and her father were getting along better. She felt like he was no longer treating her like a child, and he was actually trying to listen to her—something he refused to do before. He had been a strong shoulder to lean on when she canceled her wedding to Alonzo, who had remained a part of her son's life. They decided to work together as parents. Marriage was definitely off the table.

Maybe the therapy was working. Erica had resisted the idea at first. Then, she thought about how difficult it would be to move on and figured it was better to try to change for the sake of her son.

Her son seemed to adore his namesake. Daddy had been spending a lot of time with his grandson, and he was doing for him everything Alonzo didn't or couldn't do. They were finally behaving like a family. He would even keep the child while she was in culinary school. Her father hooked her up with a mentor, Janet Lowery, chef and owner of The Open Table. Erica ate dinner with her dad twice a week, and they would sit and talk afterward. She played it cool, but she was so excited to have the relationship with her father that she had always wanted.

Erica couldn't help thinking this newfound closeness had something to do with the fact that Veronica wasn't there. After Jose's death, she had been inconsolable. She acted like she really loved him. And who knew? Maybe Cruella had been capable of loving someone, even though it seemed unlikely given her preoccupation with her lifestyle. One thing was for sure: Daddy didn't want her anymore, and he made sure she understood that. Per their prenup, she left emptyhanded. Zip. Zilch. That alone brought a broad smile to Erica's face. The witch was gone for good.

Erica spent her days rebuilding her life, and she enjoyed the sound of little Byron's gurgle. Now she looked at him to see him smiling at her. He seemed to approve of the life she was building for him. Like her father, maybe he thought she was finally growing up.

ABOUT THE AUTHOR

Since 2012, Jaye Cheríe has used her vast experiences to build character driven stories about life, love and money. Her novels, The Golddigger's Club and The Cost of Love and Sanity were released through Simon & Schuster. She has photographed, interviewed and written articles on entertainers and personalities in pop and urban culture. Jaye Cheríe resides in Jacksonville, Florida.

Connect with Jaye

Join her email list http://eepurl.com/bylGWr

Visit her on Twitter at
https://twitter.com/jayecherie
or
Facebook at
https://www.facebook.com/pages/Jaye-Cherie/158179884335117.

IF YOU ENJOYED <u>NO MERCY</u>, READ WHERE IT ALL STARTED...

THE GOLDDIGGER'S CLUB

BY JAYE CHERÍE

CHAPTER 1

MONICA

"Hut, hut, hut." The quarterback seized the snap and stretched his arm backward, winding up for a throw. He fired the ball right into the arms of Tampa Bay Buccaneers wide receiver, Tony T. Hatcher. Tony cradled the ball and mustered all the speed and power in his six- foot- five muscular physique to sprint across the goal line. When Tony stopped running, the head coach blew his whistle. All the players broke their positions, allowing waves of sweat to run down their sculpted chests and defined biceps.

The coach hurled his roll of papers to the ground.

"What are y'all doing? If we practice like this, we'll play like this during the season. Now, pick it up!" the coach shouted. The players trudged back to their line of scrimmage to practice the drive again.

Unlike the spectators perched on the bleachers, Monica Hatcher stood on the sidelines trying to play the supportive wife, but the sweat threatening to escape from her pores made it difficult to concentrate. As she watched her husband practice, she kept lapsing into daydreams of relaxing near the pool with a glass of iced tea at her side. That's where she preferred to spend the day.

Instead, she stood tall, hastily pulling her long, black ponytail behind her shoulders. Tony loved her manufactured mane but she yearned for her cropped haircut. She vowed to return to her signature tresses, at least while the heat index topped out at 102 degrees. In the meantime, she obliged her husband with her hair and her presence at the field. Monica figured this would stop him from complaining. Lately, he had harsh words for her absence at his practices. Tony claimed she was acting like a fair-weather fan because his team had a rough season last year.

While she would admit she wasn't attending like she did when he first entered the NFL, it had nothing to do with the team's record. It was just that practice, home games, and away games got old after eight years. She'd grown tired of feigning fulfillment in the NFL life. She was also tired of moving, tired of politicking and tired of smiling big for the cameras. She wanted to focus on activities more important to her, like planning the dinner for The Hatcher Scholarship Foundation.

The coach blew his whistle for the last time. The players broke their positions as if they'd been carrying a ton of bricks they were waiting to drop. Tony jogged over to Monica, wiping the sweat off his tanned forehead. "Hey. Where the kids at?" Tony asked, out of breath.

"They're with Marianna. I would never bring them out here. Too much open space for them to run or disappear, and I'm not running them down in this heat. Do you want your son running beside you on the field?" Monica asked.

Tony jerked his head back and frowned. "No."

Between the look on Tony's face and the looks from nearby players, Monica guessed she was a little too forceful in her response.

One player walked by, appearing to scowl at her. Self-conscious, Monica glanced around, while smoothing out the wrinkles in her sleeveless dress. She thought about how another passerby might view her as a bourgeois witch, but she really wasn't that way. She didn't consider herself a shallow, irresponsible woman — -the type who let her 'help' raise her children because she was too busy shopping and partying. She did, however, believe in using nannies and cooks to help her out. But even with the extra help, her family was still priority number one for her; the children knew they could count on mommy.

A tiny bit embarrassed at her own behavior, Monica dropped her head and sighed. "I'm sorry. It's so hot out here. I think my brain is sweating."

"Well, it is spring and we are in Florida," Tony said, sarcastically. "If you got a problem with the heat, why did you come here?"

"I came out here to support you."

"And you're doing that by standing on the sidelines mean mugging?"

"I wasn't aware I was supposed to be cheesing from ear to ear. You say I never come out. So, I'm out here." Monica placed her hands on her hips.

Tony threw his head back and pushed his thumbs inside of his sleeveless shirt. "All I'm saying is don't do me any favors."

Monica squinted at him. She'd sacrificed not only her comfort, but her time to make him happy. He could have at least acted like he appreciated it. If she'd known he'd react this way, she would have stretched out at her pool, or better yet, she could have used the day to check out a couple of venues for the scholarship dinner in August.

Now that Monica thought about it, she didn't know why she thought giving him what he wanted would make any difference. Nothing seemed to please him these days, especially since the season started. She knew the reasons behind his sour behavior — his smaller contract and unfocused teammates — but it was most disturbing that his attitude was rubbing off on her. Before she could address their growing discord, Tony turned toward the stadium exit.

"Where are you going?" Monica asked.

"I'm gonna shower, pick up the kids and take them to the park," Tony said.

"Fine. I'm going to meet Dee and Stephanie for an early dinner," Monica said.

Tony rolled his eyes.

"Don't start, okay?" Monica asked. Tony didn't care for Monica's friends. They didn't like him much either. She wasn't sure how it started but she was getting real sick of playing referee.

Tony placed his hand on his chest, faking innocence. "I didn't say anything. I'll see you when you get home."

Tony jogged off the field toward the locker room. When he passed two women sitting in the stands, he winked at them. They batted their eyes back and burst into giggles. The shorter one whispered to her friend, who howled in amusement.

The acid in Monica's stomach bubbled over like a boiling pot of water. She didn't attend Tony's practice to see him flirt with other women. Before the end of the day, she planned to read him about his behavior. Annoyed, Monica walked toward the exit, eyeing the two ogling women.

During the drive to meet her friends, Monica was still pretty hot with Tony. So much so, she had to imagine the layout of the scholarship dinner to calm down. She envisioned an ice sculpture at the front entrance of the venue. Elegant crystal chandeliers in the dining area. Twenty-five tables with champagne table cloths and floral centerpieces placed at the center. She'd present a plaque along with a $25,000 check for college to two eager high school students.

Thinking about the dinner instantly put Monica at ease. By the time she reached Henrietta's Bistro, she caught herself smiling. When she entered the quaint restaurant, her friends, Deidre Wright and Stephanie Robinson, were already sitting at a booth. With the Tony incident twenty miles away, she decided to avoid bringing it up to her friends because she didn't want to ruin the positive vibe. Besides, if given the chance, they'd only use the incident as ammunition against Tony's character, which she did not feel like defending.

"Hello, ladies," Monica said.

"Hey. What's up?" Dee said, glancing up from her pocket mirror.

"Same ole, same ole. What's up with you guys? Have you ordered yet?" Monica asked.

"Yeah but here's a menu," Stephanie said, handing it to Monica.

Monica took the menu and glanced down at the choices, which included a special with collard greens, ham hocks and sweet potatoes. She shuddered to think she considered asking Henrietta to cater her dinner. Henrietta's food was savory in a soul food sort of way but she couldn't imagine serving collard greens and ham hocks to the big wigs in August. She was going to ask these CEOs and politicians for hundreds of thousands of dollars. They had to take her seriously, and to do that, she needed to produce a high class event all the way — from the venue to the food. Oh, well. Maybe I'll keep Henrietta in mind for future events, like a small birthday party. Once the waiter returned to their table, Monica ordered the four vegetable special and a tea. The waiter took her menu and she shifted her attention back to her friends.

"So, which one of you broads is gonna help me plan my dinner?" Monica asked the two women sitting across from her.

Dee looked up from her mirror with her trademark 'no, you didn't' expression. She turned around to glance at people sitting at the tables behind her. "You must be talking to someone else because I know you ain't talking to me like that."

Deidre, - or Dee to her friends, - shifted her eyes back to her pocket mirror, while fixing her wavy weave with French manicured fingers. As a fashion stylist, Dee was so appearance obsessed that she wore pricey hair, refused to leave the house without Mac makeup and shopped every week. She even liked donning hazel contact lenses and fake eye lashes. They complimented her face, she said. Today, she was minus the lashes but she maintained her diva mode with the contacts.

"Since you're so style- conscious, I thought you might be able to help me with the decoration," Monica said with a wide smile.

"I do fashion. I don't do confetti."

"You're still styling a room. When you think about it, there really isn't any difference."

"There is a difference and you know it. Now, I'm not gonna sit here and debate back and forward with you about decorations and fashions ''cuz I know nothing about the former. So, I sure hope you have something else to talk about."

Sometimes she is so impossible, Monica thought. She turned to her other friend. "What about you?"

"I would, but I'm not really fashion conscious. I don't even like those kinds of events. I mean, everybody gets all dressed up and acts like they're better than you. It gets on my nerves," Stephanie said, scrunching her round, baby face. The last rays of the setting sun shimmered over her cinnamon brown skin and long, curly hair, hinting to her Afro-Cuban lineage.

"You don't have to be fashion conscious. You can just help me make some calls. Besides, this is a dinner for a nonprofit organization. Nobody's supposed to be acting like they're better than anybody."

"You know those people aren't gonna act right," Dee said, peeking up from her mirror.

Monica shot Dee the evil eye for interrupting her volunteer campaign. I don't know," Stephanie said.

"You might meet some nice, rich men."

"When do you need help?" Stephanie asked.

"Well, I could use some help tomorrow afternoon."

"Oh, no. I have to get ready for the show. Natalie's gonna get me back stage at the Jam Fest. I already told her I would go. I need to network for more video gigs. I'm gonna spend the whole day getting ready. Sorry." Stephanie shrugged.

The waiter returned to the table with Dee's pepper steak and Stephanie's chicken fettuccine alfredo. Monica watched Stephanie divvy up the chicken chunks and sprinkle extra cheese over the pasta. It was amazing how much effort Stephanie put into the food on her plate, considering she didn't like putting effort into anything else. Whenever Monica or Dee asked her to do something - if there was any real work involved - they could forget about her. It was like she was allergic to any type of exertion. She knew Stephanie wasn't that sorry for ditching her on the dinner preparation but decided not to press the issue right then. These chicks are going to help me whether they know it or not.

"Sure. I'll let you know when I need help with something else." Monica tried her best to look dejected.

"How is the dinner going? Are you gonna use a deejay or an actual recording artist?" Dee asked, biting into a tender piece of steak.

"Well, since you don't intend to help, you're gonna have to wait and see like everybody else," Monica said, smirking.

"That's okay. It ain't that important," Dee rolled her eyes.

Monica shook her head. "Don't you want to be a part of something meaningful?"

"I'm a part of many things that are meaningful. I just think it's time for me to focus on me right now," Dee said, reaching for the barbecue sauce.

"Dang, that sounds kinda selfish," Stephanie said.

"Doesn't it?" Monica asked.

"I don't think so," Dee said. "When I said I wanted to start a fashion magazine, did any of you heifers say, 'Wow! Great, Dee! How can we help you out?'"

"We don't know anything about creating a magazine," Monica said.

"Monica, your degree is in mass communications. Even if you didn't know, I could have used your media knowledge. I could have shown you what to do, just like you were willing to show us what you needed to plan your scholarship dinner but oh, no. Instead, I was greeted with cynicism," Dee dropped her fork on her plate and crossed her arms.

"I wasn't trying to be cynical. I thought you should know magazines are losing advertising money these days," Stephanie explained.

"What did that have to do with me and my dreams?" Dee asked.

Monica raised her eyebrows and looked at Stephanie, who had a similar expression on her face. Within the past two years that they'd known each other, Dee had tried to "come up" so many times. There was the time she bought a lot of stock but ended up losing money because the companies closed or underperformed. Then, she bought real estate from a bank but lost that because she forgot to pay property taxes on it. Actually, she forgot about the property altogether. As expected, they had a hard time taking her next big thing seriously, but Dee's passion for the fashion magazine surprised Monica.

The waiter walked up to the table with Monica's special and lay it down gently in front of her. "Is there anything else I can get for you ladies?" he asked.

"No," the women said in unison.
Monica returned her attention to Dee. "Look. I'm just concerned about your abrupt change in direction," Monica said. "But I like seeing you serious about something. So, I guess that's why I need to be more supportive of your magazine. It's a good match for you, Dee. You're right. I apologize," Monica conceded. Dee smiled and pushed her chin up.

"I am too, Dee. From now on, I promise I'll be more supportive of your dreams," Stephanie added.

"Thank you, Ladies. I really appreciate it," Dee said, reaching out to touch her friends' hands.

"Now, will you help me with my dinner?" Monica asked.

Looking up at the ceiling, Dee sighed. "I'll think about it."

Visit your favorite online retailer to buy this book!